About the Author

Born and raised in southern California, Brian Lupo is the author of *Goat's Head*, a terrifying tale about a sixteen-year-old boy afflicted with anxiety panic disorder who encounters The Ones Who Dwell in the Dark. He is also a writer and director of independent horror films, *M.O.N.*, *The Sickness of Lucius Frost*, *13 Days of the Beast*, and *The Harvest*, along with several short films. He is best known for weird, psychological horror stories. He shares his California home with his wife and three dogs.

Visit him on his website at www.pulpvein.com

BRIAN LUPO

UGLY FACES

BRIAN LUPO PUBLISHING

First Printing, 2022

Cover art by David Richardson. https://www.holygoldenartpalace.com/

ISBN: 979-8-9857067-0-3

For Riana

UGLY FACES

ONE

The bell of the university rang amid a lecherous memory of ugly faces in squalid attire groping Lexi's third-grade breasts. The twenty-two-year-old tightened the hold on her black peacoat while her friend Rachael flaunted a large, sparkling engagement ring at her.

"Isn't it fantastic?"

Lexi's blue sapphire eyes stared at Rachael's phony innocence with covert distress. She could see all that concerned her was the diamond showpiece and Chad, her handsome, dark-haired fiancé, who embraced her.

"Yeah, it's gorgeous, but does this mean you're not coming with me to my parents' house?"

"That's what I wanted to talk to you about.

Chad's parents have flown out to help us coordinate the wedding—"

"So, you're not coming with me then?" The disappointment in Lexi's voice was not restrained.

Rachael's blonde heart-shaped head drew up to Chad. It was his cue to chime in.

"Look, it's my fault. I'll pay for you to fly home. No reason for you to have to drive there by yourself."

The transparent pre-rehearsed performance was an insult to Lexi's intelligence, but worse was her sense of betrayal. "You told him?"

Chad responded first, "No," and Rachael's lips compressed for a moment at his mistake.

"No, Lexi, I didn't tell him anything. I merely said you don't like to drive through open spaces. That's it."

Lexi was trembling, her tear ducts on the verge of letting loose. She glanced up at Chad, and his dark eyes fled from hers. With overt insincerity, Lexi said, "Well, congratulations, you guys. I wish you the best of luck," and turned to walk away.

"Wait."

Lexi slowed her pace, and Rachael slipped from Chad to cut her off.

"What? I have to get ready to go."

Rachael reached her hands out for Lexi to take. Lexi stole a jealous peek at the ring and remained in her self-embrace.

"I want to know if you'll be my maid of honor?"

Lexi looked straight into Rachael's amber-colored eyes, hanging on to her composure by a thread. "You tell me three hours before we're supposed to leave for my parents'—" Lexi shook her head, a tear streaming down her right cheek. "I knew you'd cancel. I knew it." She shrugged, looking off in the distance.

"How was I supposed to anticipate a proposal?"

"I would have flown home if I knew you weren't coming."

"You can fly—"

"No, I can't. I already have a rental."

"So, return it. No big deal."

Lexi could no longer hold back the tears. "You don't understand. I have to take the drive. My condition will regress otherwise." She wiped her eyes on her coat's sleeves. "This is completely unfair of you."

"Me?" Rachael crossed her arms as she leaned back.

"Yes, you."

"Unbelievable. Okay, listen." Rachael took a breather. "Tell you what. I will drive with you back to school when we resume in the spring; that way you can face your fear and not regress. How's that sound?"

"That's not how it works."

"You're impossible to please, Lexi. We offered you a flight, you don't want it. I offered to drive you back, you can't wait. What do you want from me?"

"For you to fulfill the promise you made to me to drive to my parents' house. Not that you value promises."

"What the hell's that supposed to mean?"

"You told him."

Rachael sighed, looking up and putting her hands on her curved hips. "Lexi, Chad doesn't care. He's not judging you."

"It makes no difference. It's embarrassing, and it's not your business to tell anyone. You didn't tell him about..." A fear crept into Lexi's delicate features.

"I would never."

"You told him the other."

"That's different and you know it. I would never tell him about *that*."

Lexi looked off with a sniff and broke into

tears.

"Oh, hunny, let's get you a flight."

Rachael gave her friend a hug and swatted at Chad to be patient when he gestured at his watch.

"I can't," Lexi moaned.

"Why not?"

"I just can't. I have my reasons."

Rachael looked back at the large circular clock on the library building. It read 9:06 A.M.

"I've got it. Why don't we find someone else for you to go with?"

"Like who?"

"How about Trevor?"

Lexi wiped her tears. "No. He'll turn it into something more than it is."

"So? He's cute—"

"And because he's cute, he gets a pass at taking advantage of the situation? Out of the question."

"Well... what about Grace?"

Lexi's frown lines eased. "I can try her, I guess."

"Yeah, she'll go with you."

"On three hours' notice, not likely."

"Why not? Tell her I'll give her two hundred bucks if she does."

Lexi retrieved her cell phone from her purse. "You don't have to do that. This is my problem." She stepped away from Rachael, turning her back with a distinct exhale.

"I would have spent it on a plane ticket anyway, Lex."

Lexi rolled her eyes and waved a hand back for quiet. She overheard Chad sigh and clenched her teeth. "Hey, Grace, it's Lexi. If you get this message before twelve, give me a call. Thanks, love. Talk soon, bye."

"Let me see who I can find," Rachael said, getting on her phone.

"Fuck, I'll call Trevor. I don't give a shit anymore. This is totally fucked up of you."

"I might be able to find somebody if you'll give me a minute."

Lexi shook her head at Rachael's attitude and paced to privacy.

"Hi, Trevor, I have a huge favor to ask of you." Lexi caught her pitiful reflection in a student dorm window and was propelled to get away from herself. She walked in between the dorm room buildings and stopped. "Would you be willing to drive with me to my parents' house today? You can stay over for the weekend." She felt like she was prostituting herself.

"Yeah, sure," he answered, loud and eager. "What time were you looking at leaving?"

"In—"

Lexi tried to speak, but the words would not come out. She was having trouble catching her breath. Her mind was demonstrating the many ways he could have her, without her consent. On the road, at her parents' place at night. Anywhere he could get away with it. She would be an easy target for a man of his athletic ability.

"Lexi... Lexi... are you there?... Hello, Lexi?"

With gritted teeth and features straining red to burst, Lexi hung up on Trevor and stalked off to be alone in her dorm room to think.

"Where are you going?" Rachael asked.

"I'll figure it out myself."

"We can find someone... Lexi!"

"It's not your problem. Is it?"

"Uh." Rachael threw her arms up. "Whatever, I'm done."

"Of course you are."

"Oh, grow up, Lexi. You're such a child."

TWO

Lexi's trembling hands mapped the route, time, and conditions to her parents' house in San Francisco. Rather than the usual six-and-a-half-hour drive, the app was projecting eight hours and ten minutes. A drifting stare seized her as mental images of the vast open space of Interstate 5 left her gasping for breath in the middle of nowhere. In reaction, a bestial yell uncharacteristic of her petite frame cried out as she threw her phone at her bed. She leaned against her closet door and banged the back of her skull. *I can't believe you did this to me. Of all people, you. You were never my friend. Were you?*

Her ringtone, "Punishment Fits the Crime" by the Ramones, eased the wrenching spasms in Lexi's stomach.

"Please be Grace." Lexi crawled across the floor and onto her bed, giving the caller ID a blurry glance. Getting the hair out of her eyes, she exclaimed, "*Yes.*" It was an undertaking to answer the phone as if everything was peachy. "Hi, Grace. Thanks for calling me back." Lexi spoke with near empty lungs. The feeling of passing out was ever present. "I was wondering if you'd be willing to drive with me to my parents' house today and stay the weekend with me and my folks?"

In the suspense of waiting for a reply, the sensation of hot tears dripping down from her cheeks onto her lips gave her an irritating, ticklish sensation. She licked the sweet, salty taste from her mouth and spoke with a smacking sound that punctuated her voice. "Please, please, please, I don't want to make the drive on my own... yes, San Francisco. We can go to the beach, Napa Valley, check out Chinatown. Anything you want. And I will pay for everything. What do you say? Please say yes... I will pay for your plane flight home. Don't worry about that... Rachael was supposed to... yeah, she canceled last minute because Chad proposed. She'll tell you, she will. He just proposed last night. So, can you come with me? Please...

pretty please with sugar on top... ah-h-h, *you will?*... you're the best! I love you. It'll be fun, we'll have fun... a couple hours is perfect. I'll see you soon then?... Excellent. Okay, love you, bye."

"Ah-h-h!" Lexi jumped on her bed and danced around her dorm room like she was Elisabeth Shue in the opening of the movie *Adventures in Babysitting.*

THREE

Lexi pulled away from her administrative law book to check the time on her cell phone. It was two minutes to twelve, the desired time to leave. Her family were not of the late-night sort. They went to bed early, and Lexi did not want them waiting up for her to get in. She wondered what could be taking Grace so long and got an unsettling premonition she might pull a Rachael on her last minute. She reviewed the drive time; it had increased to eight hours and twenty-one minutes. She pulled up her contacts list and hovered her thumb over Grace's name. Reasoning a call would come off too pushy, Lexi instead decided to load the car to keep her negative thoughts at bay.

On the way out of her dorm, a call stopped her in her tracks. The electric thrill that accompanies uncertainty left her with clumsy hands and she dropped her phone. Racing to pick it up, she was disappointed to read Trevor's name on the caller ID. Lexi silenced the call and yanked her bag down the dorm room hallway, saying a perfunctory goodbye to the residential advisor in passing.

Red Falls University was clearing out. As a result, Lexi found her car in student parking lot D with ease. It was a charming old campus, full of vibrant trees, kempt hedges, and varied vegetation, all of which was still in late fall colors and hadn't looked better under a bright blue sky. Lexi had missed the brilliant color palette in her rush to forget her precarious position. It had been on her original itinerary before leaving to rest a short spell under her favorite coast redwood tree in the quad, where she had spent so many days studying within its splendid shade. However, that was not to be. In loading her suitcase and bags into her silver Fiat, she didn't even bother to glance once at her surroundings.

Closing the trunk, a text message sounded in her peacoat. Lexi plunged her hand into her pocket, her eyes wide with excitement and apprehension. She eyed the initial sentence with a seizing pressure encompassing her throat.

"DON'T HATE ME. I can't go after all. I CAN'T TELL YOU HOW SORRY I AM. My mom sprung my nephew on me for the weekend and I can't get out of it. Just turn on some music for the drive and it will breeze by. I'M REALLY SORRY! I'll call you later, okay? Don't be mad at me. :("

Lexi's eyes widened further. When she was scared or nervous to no end, the whites of her eyes grew big, giving her a creepy and unbalanced look. She hated her "funny face," as the kids used to call it growing up. The kids who bullied her for being a shy introverted little girl, gifted at not making friends. She couldn't understand how, after all the therapy sessions to improve her social skills and her ability to face anxiety-filled challenges, she was here again, scared, alone, and friendless. *When will the cycle end? Am I doomed to suffer forever! Fuck! Fuck everybody! You traitors! Errahh!'* She screamed in muted silence.

What emerged from staring at her "funny faced" reflection in the trunk's window was sheer sadness, a sadness that left her wanting to give up. Then came a strength, an inexplicable strength by virtue of utter hopelessness toward the odds, and a world where pain and self-reliance was a commonplace theme. *I will not let you beat me. I will not let you control my life. I will conquer you. You son of a bitch. I will win.* There was another woman looking back at her now. A beautiful, empowered woman, who was determined to face her challenge head on. A woman who would not give in to the mental rape holding her down.

Lexi unbuttoned her coat to cool off. The top of her scalp was soaked in sweat, as was her forehead, upper lip, underarms, and palms. Using a tissue from her purse, she wiped off what perspiration she could. She went around the car, inspecting the tires. Without another thought, Lexi strode to the driver's side door and threw it open, tossing her coat and purse on the passenger side seat. She prepared to get in and hesitated with the shakes. Slowing her breathing and not letting another scared thought enter her mind, she got into her rental car as if it were a roller coaster ride. *Fast and without thinking.* She strapped in for the ride and hesitated with the ignition key. While her thoughts of the dreaded Interstate were blank at the moment, a fear was ever present in her subconscious mind. It informed her she was only fine because she was not yet on the open highway. There she would panic, and gasp for air, holler and scream for help. She'd be prey for sordid predators lurking about for an easy mark.

Lexi turned the car on, putting the gear into drive. The coaster eased on down the track, and Lexi stepped on the brakes. She covered her eyes with her hands, leaning back in a sobbing outburst. The mean thoughts pouring in convulsed her with seizures of emotion. The immense scale of trepidation was unreal. It submerged her breath and threatened to choke her unconscious. *You're not strong. You're weak and pathetic. You're shit.* She pounded the steering wheel, whining as she squirmed. She was sick and tired of always playing the part of the victim. *Stop itttttt!* Her eyes snapped open, and her breath started to regulate by degrees. *I can just follow someone through the I-Five? It's mostly farmland, so I'll follow a commuter with a squeaky clean or luxury vehicle. I'll use my best judgment, evaluate the passengers, see if they look like farmers. If they don't, they can be my company. Worst case scenario, they get off the highway to get gas. Act like I need to get gas too and continue to trail at a safe and harmless distance. And there, I'm in the clear."*

Lexi jolted up at the ingenuous idea, causing stars to shoot into her vision. "Hell, yeah. That'll work." She blinked. "That will work! Ahhh!" She hopped in her seat, screaming with giddiness. Lexi checked the drive time and was surprised to see the time had shrunk to seven hours and nineteen minutes, putting her estimated arrival time for her parents' at 7:46 P.M. She placed her phone in the cup holder next to her calming kombucha tea. With a light foot on the accelerator and a confident look out the windshield, she was back on track.

FOUR

Punk rock emanated out of Lexi's phone. She eyed the caller and an area to pull over. *Stop and you won't follow through.* Lexi tapped the screen to put Helen on speaker and stared forward. "Hi, Mom."

"Hi, sweetie. Have you left already?"

"I have. I'm on the road."

Lexi heard her father's muffled voice in the background. "Your father says hi and sends his love."

"Love you too, Daddy! See you soon!"

"Can't wait, sweetheart!"

Lexi smiled, thinking of home in an impatient exhale.

"Where are you?" Helen asked.

"I'm still in Redlands, about to get on the two

ten freeway. Mom, let me let you go. I want to preserve my battery for the drive."

"Do. We'll see you tonight—Ron, what is it? She's trying to conserve her telephone battery." Lexi laughed.

"What, Lexi?"

"You're showing your age. You called my cell phone a telephone."

"It is a telephone."

Lexi laughed and felt unexpected tears push against the backs of her eyes. She wanted to ask her parents for help. *No!*

"Your father wants me to tell you girls to be careful and to drive slow." Lexi stroked her hair back, batting her eyes not to cry. "Weather Channel's predicting rain. You know how people get in the rain. They drive like such idiots."

"Mom," Lexi didn't want to say it. "...it'll just be me coming. Rachael couldn't make it."

"Well, who's with you?"

She hesitated. "...No one."

"You're driving home by yourself?" Helen said in a sharp tone. "Lexi... "

"It'll be fine, Mom. I'm going to follow someone through the I-Five. It'll be fine."

"Lexi, I still don't—"

"Just be by your phone. I'll be alright."

"Lexi, I don't want you driving here by yourself."

Lexi squeezed her face red so as not to explode with emotion.

"Why is she driving by herself?" her father yelled with concern.

"It'll be fine, I'm fine. Seriously." A single tear ran from Lexi's right eye. *I can't tell them. I can't.*

Helen stepped away from the receiver. "Rachael couldn't come."

"Why not?" her father barked.

Lexi stretched her neck from side to side at the argument between her parents on whether or not she should be allowed to continue her drive, as if they had a decision in the matter.

"Mom, I have to go. You're running my battery down."

Helen got back on the phone. "Lexi, I don't want you driving here. Your father and I would rather you fly. We'll pay."

Lexi sleeved the tear from her flushed cheek. *Deja vu.* She huffed from frustration. "Mom, stop. I have to go. I'm entering the two ten."

"Lex—"

"Mom, stop! You're making me more

nervous."

"Mmmm... we'll be by our phone."

"I appreciate it. Love you."

"Love you. I'm not okay with this, Lexi."

"It'll be fine. Bye, Mom."

"Call if you need us."

"I will. Bye."

"…Okay, bye."

The voices of her parents faded out, still arguing. Lexi hung up. She looked out the windshield with a sigh and head shake, searching the horizon for signs of rain. The sky in every direction was a long expanse of blue as far as the eyes could see. Lexi tested the car's front and back windshield wipers and the headlights, leaving nothing to chance. All was in excellent working order. She checked her phone for a traffic update. The highway was moving up until Rialto, where it indicated moderate congestion. Her eyes went to her battery level, which registered ninety-seven percent. The three percent loss caused her to inhale with an awareness of slight failing courage, for the phone had to last 439 more miles. She cursed not having a car charger. *It's Rachael's fault. All of this is Rachael's fault.* Lexi gripped the steering wheel and squeezed the leather hard three times. There was no logical reason why she should be faltering in her courage. *The strategy is flawless*, she told herself.

Lexi put slender fingers in her mouth, trying to find a nail she could chew on that wasn't bald. There wasn't one. In reaction, she turned to biting off bits and pieces of the skin along her lateral nail folds, spitting the remnants of herself out the window as her mind went over the steps involved with making it across the interstate.

She would stop off in Castaic, taking exit 176B, Lake Hughes Road. After filling her tank at the 7-Eleven off Lake Hughes and Castaic Road, she would use the restroom if need be. Next, she would grab a bite to eat from the McDonald's right beside the freeway. There, she would wait in the parking lot for the appropriate vehicle to get on the freeway heading north. It was that simple. So, why were her thoughts telling her it wasn't too late to catch a flight home? It didn't make sense. *Plans with a high probability of success can still fail.* Lexi took Grace's advice and turned on the radio. KOLA 99.9 FM was doing an all-day 80s flashback, her favorite.

The traffic started early in San Bernardino on the Foothill Freeway west due to an accident on the shoulder, near the Rialto airport. Every lane was bumper to bumper with eager motorists edging in and out of lanes for an insignificant leap forward. The cluttered and hectic atmosphere was numbed by the music Lexi was singing to. She sang along to the likes of Cindy Lauper, Milli Vanilli, The Ramones, and Duran Duran, and was improving in mood and courage. Then, Rachael had to call and put a damper on things.

Just the name alone on the caller ID brought the taste of brake dust and the smell of exhaust pipes into Lexi's lungs. She could now see the dark clouds on the horizon. To add insult to injury, the carpool lane came into sight and was moving at a normal pace. Lexi silenced the call, gripped the wheel, and turned up the music. Unfortunately, it was the tail end of a song block, followed by a commercial break. Turning the volume down, she noticed the brick walls edging the freeway and cropping out the mountains and palm trees to her left and right. She felt like rounded-up cattle pushing forward on cracked hardtop, without so much as roadside vegetation to give a semblance of serenity to the anxious herd. Even the blue sky had faded into a polluted, grayish-white expanse.

Lexi closed her eyes for a moment and put her teeth together with a crushing pressure. She saw Rachael's engagement ring in her mind and opened her eyes with the thought, *The closest you'll ever get to love is Trevor.* Lexi quivered and shrugged off the disagreeable forecast. In doing so, a lifted truck cut her off, and she laid her palm on the horn. The man in the red Toyota Ram gave her a glare in the rearview mirror. She didn't care; she scowled back and stuck her tongue out at the driver. The driver gave her the finger in return.

Lexi found herself getting shaky with anger. She wanted to flip the man off; however, she was not in a favorable position to press her luck. The driver of the truck needed only to brake his vehicle to pin her in. Because the middle lane was not moving, and the carpool lane moving too fast, she would have no escape if the man stepped out of the vehicle for an altercation. She did have blue mace in her purse, but between being in the car and the wind outside, the chances of the mace blowing back into her vehicle was a risk not worth taking.

With a sigh of reservation, Lexi averted her eyes from the driver's back window to concentrate on the road. The act of letting the asshole get away with his power trip in his big imposing truck was intolerable. *Fuck this guy. Compensating douche bag.* Lexi's heartbeat increased with a want for revenge. She watched the carpool lane for a gap large enough to gain the speed necessary to slip in without cutting someone off, like this asshole did her.

The line of speeding cars had no current perceivable end. Lexi gripped the wheel, the pit of her stomach aching. She saw a couple openings that she might have been able to squeeze into but lost her nerve at the last second. A minute later, her opportunity came. She went to gas it, and the truck in front of her came to a sudden and complete stop. She had to brake and lost her opening. "Fuck!" Lexi hit her steering wheel. Something in her leaden mind said to look at the driver. She did. He was laughing, as if he knew what she'd attempted and braked on purpose. The truck's width made it impossible to see past the vehicle to confirm if Lexi's suspicion was correct. *Why else would he be laughing?*

Someone in the three lanes of inching traffic began blasting rap music. Lexi's body thumped from the excessive vibrations. She looked around for the aggravating vehicle and couldn't locate it. It could have been one of many obnoxious candidates. Lexi despised hardcore rap; the way it presented and spoke about women as pieces of ass-flapping meat upset her. Her index finger pulled on the white collar popping out of her blue sweater. The urge to make an aggressive maneuver into the carpool lane was accentuated when she noticed the truck's license plate. It read, "My Beast." *What a piece of crap.*

Lexi gave the carpool lane a glance. There was no space, no time to zip in. She was getting desperate. A sense of claustrophobia was building in the tightness of the little Fiat. She was trapped, the interior of the vehicle compressing with the acceleration of her heart rate, squeezing the sweat out of her pores.

The music on the radio returned with the song "Gloria" by Laura Branigan. Lexi turned up the volume to compete with the rap, hoping it would ease her anxiety. It was no use. Laura's lyrics were accompanied by an annoying bass-filled thumping beat and deep male voice saying motherfucker-this and motherfucker-that. Lexi felt the car becoming a furnace and turned on the air conditioner. Giving the carpool lane another glance, she spotted a sudden gap. She floored the gas and swung into the lane with a hard, sharp jerk on the steering wheel. A car was at her back in seconds. Lexi flipped off the truck driver while blowing past. The bro in the driver's seat threw his hands up, and Lexi laughed at him, waving goodbye.

Leaving the shithead and terrible music in her dust brought a smile to Lexi's thin lips. She watched the incalculable motorists stuck in single-rider lanes flow backward at a speed of fifty-five miles per hour. *He'll never catch up,* she thought, peering back to see if he'd gotten into the fast lane. He hadn't from what she could see, and given his vehicle's height, he would have been obvious in the line-up of smaller compact cars.

Lexi turned the radio down and the air conditioner off, feeling her body shakes begin to ebb. She looked out for cops and cracked her window when she didn't see any. The breeze flowed throughout her soft, long hair. It was a refreshing sensation that compelled her fingers to stroke the crown of her head. Her scalp tingled to the touch and prompted her to release a relaxing purr. Lexi listened to the sound of swiping traffic to her right. It was music to her ears. It signaled putting continual distance between her and that awful scene back there.

For miles, the carpool lane maintained its speed. Then, as the accident approached, the lane slowed to a rubbernecking pace. Lexi predicted the police would be too busy with the accident to notice her trivial infraction, and she could just coast by. Not that she wasn't prepared to accept a ticket for her violation in the event she was caught—she was, and the price was worth the risk. Not that she wouldn't attempt to talk herself out of it—she would, using the threat of road rage as her alibi. What worried her was being pulled over and having the truck drive by and see her getting into trouble. It would put the position of power back in the jerk's favor. That she could not have. She would have to tell the officer that it was that man who raged on her, so he would get in trouble also. A tremendous time suck she'd rather avoid if at all possible.

Like the others, Lexi couldn't ignore viewing the crash site. The accident was terrible. A brown four door had run into the steel bed of a tow truck, flattening the front end of the vehicle. Firefighters were on the passenger side of the car with the jaws of life, attempting to get what Lexi gathered was a passenger out of the back seat. She had to wonder if it was not a child. The thought caused her throat to tighten. There had been a sheet placed over the car's front windows to hide the gore. Lexi glimpsed a bloody arm hanging out of the driver's side window when the sheet swept up from a fleeting gust of wind. The occupant inside was slumped forward on the dashboard, the head twisted at an unnatural angle. It was a sight Lexi wished she hadn't seen. She spotted the tow truck driver farther up the highway, evident by his uniform. He was sitting on the shoulder in hysterics, talking to three police officers without evident injury.

A bad omen, she thought. *A bad omen.* Lexi turned up the radio and got out of the carpool lane.

FIVE

By Monrovia, rows of gray clouds were drifting overhead, sprinkling the Fiat with sporadic showers. By the outskirts of Pasadena, the mountains were murky outlines and the highway sodden with shoulder flooding. Lexi tried not to let the worsening conditions get to her. It was difficult, considering she was stuck in another pocket of traffic, moving at a speed of fifteen miles per hour.

Lexi's phone rang and the caller ID displayed "Mom." She put the call on speaker.

"Mom, whatcha need? I'm in traffic."

"Where are you?"

"Pasadena, why?" Lexi said, with a hint of irritation.

"Your father and I talked. We'd prefer you to

fly home. There's a flight—"

"No, Mom!"

"Lexi, there's a storm heading your way and we don't want you getting caught in it."

"Too late, I'm in it, and it's not that bad. Now Mom, I have to let you go; you're draining my battery."

A call from Rachael came in on Lexi's other line and she glared at the phone, pushing the straight-to-voicemail button.

"She says she's in the storm," Helen said to Ron in the background.

Ron said something.

"Lexi, how's the weather?"

"Raining."

"Severe rain?"

"No, regular rain. I'll be fine, Mom. I have to go. I will call you if I have any issues."

"Promise?"

Lexi's rude tone vanished. "Yes, I promise."

"Your father wants you to turn around immediately if the weather becomes rough."

A few lines of the intro ballad of "Gilligan's Island" played in Lexi's head, forcing a quick laugh. *The weather started getting rough, the tiny ship was tossed. If not for the courage of the fearless crew, the*

Minnow would be lost.

"I will."

"We'll be by our phone."

"Thank you. Bye, Mom."

Helen sighed. "Bye."

Lexi glanced at her phone's battery. It was at 87 percent and she still had 383 miles to go. "Fuck, stop calling me. *God damn it,*" she murmured, gripping the steering wheel hard. Taking a drink of kombucha, she relied on the I-theanine to balance her mood. The sweet taste of strawberry, watermelon, and banana brought on fleeting respite. She was getting an aching pressure in her temples, running down along her teeth. Lexi stretched her neck from side to side, and it cracked at the base of her skull in both directions. *I could really use someone to push on my back.* She shifted forward and pinched her shoulder blades behind her to ease the dull, aching pressure on her spine.

The rain reduced in Pasadena, drizzling over the scurrying traffic. Everyone was in a rush to beat the dimming clouds home before they burst open in a downpour. The sky was a looming time bomb releasing periodic showers until La

Crescenta, where a torrent was unloaded on the Fiat amid the desolate foggy hills of La Tuna Canyon.

Lexi made her way up the sinuous highway and grew stiff in posture. Upon rounding a blind curve, she was forced to a complete stop. All four lanes of traffic were jammed full of stalled commuters, resting in a lazy mist. For Lexi, there was only one thing more terrifying than driving alone in a complete desolate area, and that was being in a desolate area where traffic was not moving. She did not expect this part of the freeway to be packed. The weather had complicated matters. She checked her app for how long the delay would last. The roots of her hair pulled upward as she rested her enlarged white eyes on a canyon route marked in solid red.

"No, no, no," she whined in desperation, forgetting the Beastie Boys song she was singing. Her funny face eyed the flooded emergency lane, glazed over in a pale, clammy stare. The traffic accident she'd seen flashed in her head to caution her impulse to enter the lane. Lexi glanced at the unoccupied hills half shrouded in clouds. The sight created the sensation of wanting out of her skin and to run into those bosky hillsides, screaming for the closest area of development. The abandonment of reason brought forth a moaning cry and an emphasis for immediate escape. She attempted to swallow, and the air got caught in her throat. Her hands went at her neck to scratch the air bubble down so she could breathe. When it didn't happen, she cried out in a mini yelp of sheer panic and reached for the kombucha. She spilled the drink from her shaking hands as she brought it to her bloodless lips to dislodge the obstruction. The kombucha went down the wrong hole, and Lexi coughed up the liquid onto the passenger-side floor.

What ensued was a plea in the form of a scream birthed out of self-asphyxiation. The sound tore into the lack of ventilation present in the car. Lexi gripped the steering wheel with wet hands and gunned the little silver bullet into the emergency lane. The rain assailed her windshield, making it difficult to monitor the narrow borders of the lane. Also thwarting her need for suicidal speed was the water fighting against the tires, kicking up around her side windows as the pressure wrenched her car toward the stalled motorists on her right.

"This is your fault, Rachael! Your fault, you liar! How could you do this to me? You're supposed to be my friend."

Lexi strangled the steering wheel, shaking it back and forth while shedding tears. She could hear the angry motorists honking at her and didn't blame them for protesting. She imagined their glares. "I'm sorry, okay," she shouted at them. "It's not my fault. It's not."

Left nearsighted by the elements, a set of conceivable terrors clamped down on Lexi's shoulders and held her rigid in her seat. She thought of someone broken down in her path, or a piece of vehicle debris getting caught in the undercarriage of the Fiat and rendering her rental disabled, or a police officer pulling into the lane behind her and making her stop, or even an asshole putting his vehicle into the lane to keep her from passing. She did her damnedest not to think at all, but it was no use; the fears were ever flowing in a constant cycle of breathtaking uncertainty.

The wheels jerked hard to the left and Lexi was thrown toward the concrete median. "Ahhh!" she screamed, pulling out of the near miss by millimeters. *Crash and it's over*, she told herself. Her heart's pounding mounted into a stampede as she eased back on the accelerator out of necessity. It was impossible to tell if the tremors felt in the car were not hers and hers alone. Every muscle was concentrated on the road. *How much farther?* she repeated between thoughts of worst-case scenarios.

The sound of traffic on the opposite side of the freeway mocked her as it blew by with swishing sounds. Lexi's lower jaw went crooked and stuck in that position. She leaned forward, searching for an end to her torture. There was no time to look at road signs, nor her phone to get a sense of where she was. If not for her continuing to have the freedom to drive, it was her belief that she would lose her sanity.

Lexi's phone rang, and she was thrilled to find the distraction had afforded her some room to breathe. She gave the caller's identity a glimpse, and the road and its seemingly endless winding path appeared less insurmountable. She could once again hear the radio. The song "Who Made Who" by AC/DC was playing. Fortunately for Lexi, the canyon was, in reality, a short distance. It had been the elements that distorted the environment's true length. Once she reached Sunland Boulevard, houses and businesses began to form out of the whitening mist. Feeling stupid because of her condition, Lexi pulled back into regular traffic with her head lowered from the other commuters. The pink of her ivory complexion drew back into her skin. With no interest in having an apologetic conversation regarding the specifics of how Grace invariably got locked into babysitting her nephew, Lexi cleared the missed call off her phone's screen and put her focus back on the creeping highway.

It was near Osborne Street when the source of the pile-up was revealed. A man and his family were broken down in the second lane with their flashers on. The poor man was under the hood, working to get his Toyota Rav4 off the highway. It was a miserable scene. *Sucks. Better here, though, than in the canyon,* Lexi thought, driving by.

With the unexpected crowds of La Tuna Canyon, Lexi worried about the longer desolate pass leading into Interstate 5 North to Santa Clarita. She kept her composure, figuring she'd ride in the emergency lane if the situation called for it. What really bothered her were the drivers when she did traverse the freeway exchange. They were, as her mother put it, driving like complete idiots. To her advantage, the freeway was mainly open. Still, Lexi couldn't help rocking in her seat, uneasy from the memory of the previous pass.

It was the music that once again got her through.

The weather over Valencia was disconcerting, the clouds graying into traces of black. The soaring roller coasters of Six Flags Magic Mountain were tracks suspended in a dense fog. The theme park signaled the Lake Hughes exit was closing in. Lexi could hear the screams of the ride goers as they were whipped downward from midair plummets. She imagined, against her will, that they were her own screams.

A mental projection of the desolate highway ahead shifted her in her seat. The unbidden thoughts of gasping in her car all alone were unkind and nonstop. With total visual focus on the highway, she went to retrieve her cell phone to check the battery life and pulled back with a sudden apprehension. *No, leave it be. In fact, turn it off.* Lexi shut her phone off to conserve the battery. She wondered if her parents would think something was wrong. *It's not too late to turn around for LAX.* Lexi yanked hard on her seat belt to ease the annoying sensation of being held down. Two men with ugly faces entered her mind, and she gripped the wheel until the bones of her hands threatened to pop out of the flesh. In a significant exhale, she said with clenched teeth, "You can do this… stop it, you can, and you will."

SIX

The Lake Hughes Road sign drew into sight. Lexi sat up in her seat and swallowed over the ball in her throat. Biting off slivers of skin beside her nails, she watched the exit sign drift over the car. She glanced down the highway at her tangible nightmare come to life. The highway communicated its emptiness by opening into inundated hillsides of isolation, made worse by its equal stretch from thereon into foggy depths. To further burden her negative thoughts, a mere two delivery trucks occupied the road. Neither was of any use to follow. She didn't trust truckers; they were a dicey bunch and mostly male. With a look back in the rearview mirror, she shuddered to see there was no one there, only fog and rain. Her eyes strayed from the miserable future and locked on to the golden arches of McDonald's. A warm sensation abated the cold atmosphere, infecting the Fiat's interior. The arches let Lexi know she was not yet alone.

Making a right off the freeway, she made a straight line for the 7-Eleven not a quarter block down the road. She pulled up to pump number four and stepped out of the vehicle with a shiver. The rain was pouring off the canopy, spritzing her. Brushing her sprinkled hair back, she put on her coat and hugged herself. Lexi did not want to wait in the car while the tank was filling, knowing she would be sitting for the next five hours or more. Her stiff legs appreciated the break. She leaned forward against her rental and surveyed her lonely surroundings, listening. The rain fall sounded like applause, and she imagined it was for her for having come this far. She peered at the young man reading a magazine in the 7-Eleven behind the cashier's desk and then at a family of three sitting in Fosters Freeze next door. She looked down, missing her parents and wishing they were together. She wondered if that family was heading in her direction. They were an ideal fit to follow, happy and loving and all smiles.

For some ill reason, Lexi looked north in her

head. She was trapped with a mental picture of herself not breathing. She looked wide-eyed and giddy at the nothing in every direction, fighting for air in her smothering Fiat. A gust of wind sprayed Lexi down, stealing her breath in present time. She let out a stifled shout from the thrill of the icy slap. After a minute of rigid panting, she was able to re-claim herself from the awful daydream. When she had shouted, her teeth had stamped one another with a pressure she thought would have cut her tongue off. She rolled her tongue in her mouth to verify it was still there, shaking her head at the thought of what damage she could have done.

She went to remove the nozzle from her gas tank and spotted it. The old, rusted Ford was something out of a backwoods horror film. Lexi eyed the family next door, then the heap stuck at a red light. She was frozen with indecision. Everything would depend on where the rust bucket was headed next. It had come from the direction of the freeway. Lexi got a dreadful psychic intimation that the heap was heading in her direction to gas up at her station. The very real possibility caused the blood in her veins to chill.

Lexi felt drool on the corner of her lip and sleeved it dry. She took to hiding behind the pump's body, as a sickness turned in her stomach. The Ford stalked forward on uncapped, bald tires of different widths. The front grill was bent into a crooked mouth. Out of the four headlights, the front light on the right side was missing. Lexi traced two large silhouettes in the vehicle and could swear they were watching her despite her covering. Another gust of wind sprayed her, and she squirmed from top to bottom, visualizing two pairs of stained black hands. She recalled the scent of trash on their fingers. An urge to puke gripped her. At once, she was compelled to remove the nozzle from her gas tank, but that would put her in full view of the truck. She looked at the family in Fosters Freeze and saw with even wider eyes that they were getting ready to leave. Lexi's chest rose and fell in rapid succession to the point where her heart hurt.

She peered between the pumps and could make out the two occupants. They were both men, dumb and ugly in appearance. She ran to the rear tire of the Fiat and yanked out the hose. Casting back circumspect glances over her shoulder, she saw the passenger point at her, referencing the driver to have "a look see" at the pretty little thing. Lexi felt her forehead burst with perspiration. She left her receipt in the machine, racing for the driver's side door. She jerked the car open, jumped inside, and started the engine, slamming the door shut. The rusty truck drove right past the station and out of sight, heading east. Lexi stared a moment, then fell back against her headrest with a hand to her head and had a good laugh at herself. *You paranoid bitch.* She sighed in relief, letting her pounding heart slow. She looked in the rearview for the whereabouts of the family, spotting them in the Fosters Freeze parking lot, getting into their family van.

Lexi was willing to skip lunch to gain this advantage in her favor. To her disappointment, the family made a left on Castiac Road, heading south. She got the impulse to look at the cashier in 7-Eleven. The young man was eyeing her with an all too familiar look, the look of a mental patient who was contagious. *He saw the whole thing.* Embarrassment flushed her pale complexion with a vivid redness. She looked forward and drove away from the judgment.

They could be waiting for you to leave. She gave a thorough inspection of Lake Hughes Road to the east before pulling out and heading west for McDonald's.

Lexi threw away the sticky bottle of kombucha outside McDonald's and went inside to use the restroom. The ordeal with the two ugly-faced men had put a heavy pressure on her bladder. The fast-food joint and its play area were without customers. Lexi ordered a cheeseburger, fries, and bottled water to go and asked for the bathroom key.

The teenage brunette managing the orders gave her several concerned observations during their transaction, almost as if she was inclined to ask her if she was okay. The reason became apparent in the bathroom mirror as Lexi washed off the layers of sweat and angst from her reflection. The drive and the close call at the gas station had given her the appearance of a battered woman. Her eyes wore red and dark puffy circles, and her skin was distressed and free of color. In fixing her hair, she came across an alarming sight. Out of her abundant long, starry black strands, she pinched a single white hair. She scrutinized the indication of death and thought, *You're killing yourself. You do know that, right?* Lexi got the urge to cry and recovered herself with an effort. "I can't live like this anymore," she whispered. She wadded up the tissues in her hand and threw them into the trash. She touched up her makeup and gave her improved aspect a once over before leaving the restroom.

Lexi sat facing the opposite way of the brunette cashier while waiting for her food. She crossed her hands on the table and sat as composed as she could. She figured the brunette was watching her and did not want to be hassled with nosy questions. Looking forward at the play area, she pretended the I-5 north out the window on her right did not exist. It was difficult to tune out what was behind her while also endeavoring to tune out what was to come. She wished she had her phone to keep her mind occupied; she would have watched her favorite program, *Monk*. The character Adrian Monk's excessive compulsive disorder always made her feel a tad less odd in the world. Lexi's left leg began fidgeting at the uncomfortable insecurities sneaking into her head. Next thing she knew, her order was called. She collected her food, averting eye contact with the brunette, and said, "Thank you."

Protecting her order with her coat, she ran to get into her rental. She placed the tasty smelling bag on the passenger seat and saw the juice stains from her coughed-up drink. It set her wondering a moment what the cleaning bill was going to be. "Fuckin'-A, you klutz. Can't you do anything right?" She shook her head, frowning at the varied droplets, and took out her apprehension in the form of anger towards the minor mishap. Placing her hands on the wheel, she felt a sticky residue. *I bet the floor's all sticky too, dammit*! She wet some napkins with her water bottle and wiped down the steering wheel. *Be more careful!*

Lexi leaned back, closed her eyes, and took a deep breath. She realized she was overreacting and resolved to calm down by keeping her eyes closed and focusing on a series of steady breaths. After gaining enough composure to move on, she drove her car to the closest parking spot that edged the exit of McDonald's to search for a candidate to follow. Her gaze traveled the empty Lake Hughes Road. With a start, Lexi's blood froze. The men's obscene intentions were prominent on their ugly faces. She clocked the unbelievable sight like it was a cruel illusion apt to disappear. The rusted truck was parked at the 7-Eleven gas station. The two men in their hunting attire were tracking their prey in conspiratorial observation as they gassed up.

Burgeoning on a panic attack, a bright idea arose, though she was unsure if she had the courage to pull it off. Lexi stared at the men with nerve endings strained into erect needles. With a pulse visible in her neck, she pulled out of the parking spot and drove onto Lake Hughes Road, making an illegal left around a center divider. The vile twosome shared a wary look. Lexi made a right onto Castaic Road. The men drew towards the doors of their truck with some words, not taking their eyes off the Fiat. Lexi pulled into the Fosters Freeze parking lot, parking her car backwards to face them head on. She placed her trembling cell phone to her ear, pointing at both men and speaking with lips easy to read even with the rain. "Hello, police."

The men got in their truck and sped off. The bucket of bolts exited with such force the shocks of the vehicle let out a discordant screech. The vintage motor rattled, being pushed to its limits. The men did not look at Lexi this time. She stalked the fleeing heap until it was on the I-5 north. With no way of turning around for many, many, miles, Lexi smiled. A victorious gleam flickered in the blue sapphire of her shrinking eyes. She placed her cell phone, still off, back in the cup holder and laughed as her natural beauty was restored.

Lexi ate her food in the parking lot of Fosters Freeze, just in case the ugly-faced men decided to pull off the highway and wait for her. For twenty-five minutes she watched the freeway entrance, listening to her nose wheeze from inflammation. She contemplated every possible scenario she would encounter on the highway. She would not have the distraction of the radio to keep her company. The drive would require total concentration.

Convinced the men had moved on, she drove over to McDonald's and parked in the exact same spot as before. Lexi searched Lake Hughes Road. As before, the road was empty. To her additional dismay, the rain was escalating in force, and the fog drew inward over Castiac, limiting visibility to the east and west. She tried not to think of the time lost. After fifteen minutes went by with no sign of life, Lexi began to cry out, "Come on, come on...what the fuck, man. I have to get home." Five minutes later, she felt like tearing her hair out. Her teeth were on edge, and she was ready to start hitting everything in the car within reach.

Castaic was a ghost town. "Ahhh!" she

screamed, shaking herself and the steering wheel. "Come on already! I have to gooowa!" A maroon sedan appeared from the fog, exiting the freeway. Lexi palmed a tear off her left cheek and crossed her fingers the sedan was here to gas up for the I-5 north. The vehicle made a left up Castiac Road. "You fucking bastard! Why are you doing this to me? Why? What have I done to you?" she yelled into the roof of her rental. "Ahhh!" Lexi squeezed the steering wheel with sweaty, clammy hands. Then she paused, her eyes raising to stare a moment out of the drowning windshield. Her features grew slack. "I can't do this. I can't... I'm done." She continued looking ahead at nothing for several minutes, contemplating the price of quitting. Accepting her fate, all she could say was, "I guess that's that."

Pulling out of the McDonald's parking lot, a welling sadness put pressure behind Lexi's pulsating eyes. She didn't dare look at the I-5 north for fear a breakdown would overcome her. She made a right on Lake Hughes Road for the I-5 south. Near the overpass, a large vehicle sounded, accompanied by a silhouette driving overhead. Without thinking, Lexi stopped the car mid-road, shifted into reverse, and drove backwards to the I-5 north entrance. She set her sights on a well-cared-for white SUV. A sweet-looking boy was in the back seat. In an instant, she whipped the Fiat onto the I-5 north, taking chase.

SEVEN

It had been less than two miles into the foggy canyon when the storm let loose with a steady, persistent fury. Lexi turned on her cell phone for emotional support. Her phone signaled she had a voicemail, though she was not in a position to check the message. At present, she was leaning inward, locked on to her steering wheel, watching the SUV closely. The fog blanketing the highway had demanded she stay no farther than twenty feet away. She tried to pretend the dusky hillsides deprived of development and flooding the highway's edges were not so. Anytime she failed to, a perverse notion would slip in; the idea that she could break down at any moment and be at the mercy of utter hell.

To her pleasant surprise, a pair of headlights

appeared on her right. Lexi glanced at a car neighboring her bumper in the right middle lane. The sight brought out a confident smile. Considering the car did not deviate in speed or position, Lexi had to wonder if the driver was not clinging to her for company. It was a comforting thought, having another like her. Lexi sat back, relieving some of the pressure in her chest she didn't even know she was carrying. She breathed easier, taking in the mild humidity adhering itself to the Fiat's interior. She was tempted to try the radio and thought better of dropping her guard. *That's when mistakes can happen.* With a deep breath, she focused on maintaining hyper-vigilance.

The highway weaved through hills that raised and lowered with murky thickets. The safe speed to travel was between twenty-five and forty-five miles per hour. It was easy to let the mind wander in this climate when forced to move at this speed. It was the gloomy weather combined with the rain's hypnotic rhythm that brought out the children to play from Lexi's subconscious. She saw herself spying on them at school and from her living room window as a child, their carefree disposition filling her with utmost jealousy. Her brain then switched to Rachael's engagement ring and Chad embracing her. She mused what it must feel like to want someone to hold you; it looked very much like something she wanted to attempt. She fantasized about Chad holding her instead of Rachael.

"Let the punishment fit the crime!" The ringtone startled Lexi out of her aroused state. A quick tilt of her eyes showed it was her mom. She felt out the speaker button.

"Yeah, Mom?"

"Lexi, are you alright?"

"Yes, I'm fine. I'm following two people on the I-5."

"Yes, she's alright. She's on the five following two cars," Helen said to Ron in the background. "I was worried. I was calling you and getting your voicemail."

"I had my phone off to save the battery for the open areas."

"Oh, well, we just wanted to check on you."

Lexi frowned. Her mother's warm voice had produced an acute desire for home. "I'm fine."

"Whereabouts are you?"

"Not sure. I have a ways to go yet."

"And the weather?"

"It's not bad." She lied for her parents' sake.

"But let me let you go."

"Okay. Be careful. We are on our phone if you need us."

"Thanks, Mom. Love you."

"Love you too, sweetheart."

"Bye."

Helen hesitated. "...Bye."

The fog had gained elevation everywhere, floating over both sides of the highway and bringing down the speed to a steady thirty miles per hour. Its floating clouds of eerie vapor were so thick that the wayside hills were buried into faint contours. *I should have gone back,* Lexi thought. She made a sharp exhale and swiped strands of hair falling over her straining eyes. She glanced at the car to her rear to verify that its position had not changed. It hadn't. *The storm's a blessing in disguise.* She attempted to smile and couldn't.

Soon after, a brisk unexpected rush of water doused Lexi's windshield. Her hands re-gripped the steering wheel, protruding the bones in her hands. She ducked to look under the blurriest parts of her view. The wipers were on full blast and did not leave her blind for long. She looked at the bleak sky.

The swollen twilight ceiling promised further unexpected dousing. Lexi lifted in her seat, licked her dry lips, and let out a hampered breath.

When the wind started in, it was perceived as a fortunate turn of events, considering it lowered the prominence of the fog. Except it also pushed on the Fiat at intervals. Strong gales would tug on the tire's tread to the left. One push in particular was more akin to a shove. Lexi released a small yelp, feeling her vehicle cross into the next lane. Her mind yelled at her for not turning back when she had the chance. She glanced at the other vehicles to get a pulse on her company's disposition. However, not a single individual was observable beyond their shaded torsos. Lexi's phone rang; it was Rachael. She was about to scream, "stop calling me!" when beads of sweat surfaced out of her tensed forehead.

The sight rendered her dumbstruck.

From out of the fog the rusted truck formed, easing backward. Lexi reduced her speed, the hairs on her skin crawling. The commuters must have sensed the danger, for they slowed as well.

With the reduction of speed, the truck

disappeared back into the fog. Lexi went a trifle slower, her companions staying with her. It appeared they were sticking out the course together. Lexi winced with a want to cry. She was grateful beyond measure not to be alone out here, especially with the sick intentions of those ugly-faced bastards. Together, she could function free of panic and keep her mindset straight for a fight, if necessary.

They were waiting for me. I knew it. I fucking knew it. She nodded, silencing Rachael's annoying persistence to get a hold of her. The Fiat jerked left. Lexi drew down on the steering wheel, straightening the tires. The highway went on, treacherous with every gale force shove. She watched the fog for the truck's return, swallowing repeatedly to keep the saliva circulating in her throat. The truck was nowhere to be seen. Her gut told her they would meet again. The question was, *when.*

After what felt like a lifetime of battling the elements and anticipating the lurking truck, true fortune struck. The wind softened, as did the rain. Both a miracle and an advantage. Lexi grew giddy with excitement. Her entire anatomy squeezed to burst, leading to a squeal of growing success. With every passing mile, her goal of getting home was becoming actualized, and she would have done it on her own. *Imagine that.* It was a huge leap forward in her psychological recovery. Lexi thought of her therapist. *If only Vanessa could see me now, she'd freak.*

With the positive break in the weather, the SUV suggested a desire to speed up. Lexi believed under the current conditions they could out-maneuver the rusted heap and gain the lead. Lexi kept an eye on the car to her rear, making sure everyone was on board to increase speed. The car was maintaining her acceleration. *Let's dust these fuckers.*

Within ten minutes, the rain was back. Not as harsh as it was, but strong enough to slow Lexi and her companions' pace below forty-five miles per hour. The race to find and pass the truck had failed. Not once did Lexi get even the slightest glimpse of the rotting vehicle. Under the circumstances, she was baffled how the hunk of junk had maintained such a commanding lead. She contemplated a turn off she hadn't seen and was convinced that had to be the answer. *They probably have a shack out there, where they take their girls.* She glanced at the foggy hills and cringed at the thick, wet solitude. *They deserve to die,* she thought in a low voice in her head.

Ugly faces drew over Lexi in her mind, their mouths parted and hands at the ready for groping. Her chest heaved in and out. "I should fucking kill them," she exclaimed in an outburst. *Relax, I'm going home, I'm going home. Now is not the time to lose my shit. Not out here. I can't. I'll die. I'm almost home. Set a meeting with Vanessa on Monday and we'll work it out. Just relax.* Lexi tried to swallow and couldn't. She whined from a mini panic, becoming unseated from a lack of air. Then, the saliva went down. Lexi took a drink of water, breathing through her nose what little she could and out her mouth. It took a while, but she was able to reset by focusing on the rise and fall of her breathing.

Just when she had become calm, the unthinkable occurred. The SUV moved into the slow lane, signaling an exit off the freeway. There was a lone gas station coming up. Lexi did not know how to react, staying in the third lane. She verified her rear companion was staying put. It appeared so. She was compelled to get off the freeway. They were a team, after all. She went to signal her blinker when a wavering thought stalled her hand. *The men could be waiting for me at the station... They could be waiting for me on the road. If they're not, though, it could be a huge distance provider.* Lexi's eyes oscillated with trepidation. *The weather's not to be toyed with, and I have to get home. At least here, I'm in control. What do I do? I don't know what to do. Think, God damn it. C'mon, think, think.* Lexi knocked on her right temple for the solution. *Why didn't you gas up in Castiac like I did? Fuck. You're fucking everything up.*

It was too late. The SUV exited the highway. Lexi glanced at the worried family in the vehicle as she passed them by. *I'm a coward. I could turn back around. That's insane, c'mon. Be realistic. Plus, I don't want to abandon the car following me. Well, they're not alone; they have cell phones. They'll be fine.* Lexi squirmed in her seat, trying to make her decision sit well. *I should have exited. It's too late.* She looked back at her companion. *Please don't leave me. Aw fuck, I should have exited. Man, what the fuck, why didn't I? They would have protected me. I don't know that. I don't know that for sure. Say they hadn't, then what? I did the right thing. ...Yes.* Lexi gazed out the windshield, wondering if somewhere ahead of her, behind that curtain of gloom, there wasn't a rusted menace plotting its return.

EIGHT

exi's guilt for abandoning the SUV was short lived. As she predicted, the weather was not to be toyed with. Sailing sheets of rain, blended with broken tree limbs and uprooted vegetation, were thrown at the Fiat in periodic sweeps of wind. To add to her and her companions' trials, a thunderstorm was approaching. The clouds beyond the fog were slashed open with bolts of electricity, accompanied by a subsequent tremor that rolled out across the land.

Under the volatile conditions, the concern over the rusted truck reappearing was fading fast. Lexi was convinced the decrepit vehicle would be pulled apart in this environment. While she thought this, the Fiat was yanked to the left, and

Lexi let out a laugh in lieu of a holler for help. She was wearing a mask of imitation courage and it was waning at the edges. Lexi sleeved her sweaty upper lip. She wished she could climb into the back seat of her companion's car and lay there until they were free of the surrounding hillsides.

Screwing with her further, it was beginning to look like evening outside. Lexi did not want to know the time. It terrified her to consider she could be caught in this mess after dark. At that instant, a cold chill ran down her spine. *The brights*! Lexi had tested the headlights but not the brights. She was quick to prove they worked. She exhaled in a half whistle, pulling her restrictive collar forward. *Thank you.*

The clouds flickered with bolts of lightning, and the wind soughed over a rumbling ground. Lexi heard the screech of a hawk in the murky depths straight ahead of her and thought, *Poor creature*. However, she was wrong. It was no hawk in distress. The intermittent screeching took on the harsh sound of grinding metal. Within an instant, the rusted truck emerged from the fog, turning in a discordant skid for the Fiat's bumper. The two went face to face, the men exhibiting a panic of their own. Lexi shrank back for the impact, her arms pulling up for protection. The Fiat was yanked left, taking her hands-free wheel for a ride. The impact came from the right side. Lexi's next action was born out of instinct. She grabbed the wheel in a death grip and screamed, turning towards the middle lanes. Everything was a blur after that, and it wasn't clear if she was heading in the right direction. The highway was a cacophony of evasive maneuvers. Everyone's terror was merging, and it was impossible to tell which noises were human and which noises were machine.

Lexi found herself hydroplaning towards the right side of the road. She twisted the steering wheel in a haphazard manner, stomping on the brakes. The world became a spinning top filled with screams. When the Fiat's rotation slowed, she saw her companion veer off in a turn and the rusted truck ice skate out of control down the highway. Water sprayed the windows. Then her companion was visible again, when with a sudden jerk, she came to a halt. A shaking Lexi drew up in her seat, her eyes attempting to slow the Earth's escalated rotation. Her first thought was for the welfare of her companion. She eyed the car for signs of life. There was movement in the driver's side and passenger seats, and the brown car appeared undamaged from the front.

Lexi did a brief assessment of her whereabouts on the highway and realized she was facing the wrong direction. She had hit the guard railing by her rear left tire and found that part of the back side of her vehicle was submerged in the shoulder flooding. "Don't be caught. Please, don't be caught. Or flat, shit no, don't be flat. Don't even think about it," she said to the car, pushing the gas with a measured pressure. The Fiat's engine struggled, kicking up water. "Owww, c'mon. Don't do this to me, no. Please, no, you can't." The Fiat pulled forward in a releasing lurch. "Yes. Thank you!" Lexi shivered and turned the wheel right, driving into the second middle lane before performing a one-eighty. Her companion was at her bumper, waiting to get going when she righted the vehicle. Lexi gave a thumbs up to the back window, uncertain her companions could see her gesture of camaraderie.

Pressing the gas, Lexi received a rush of endorphins, compelling her to give a giddy squeal of survival and squirm in her seat to remove the permeating energy stirring under her skin for release. "Ahhh!" she yelled with a wide mouth, like that of a wild cat. She felt like an animal, stuck in a tiny cage. A brief glimpse in the rearview mirror displayed a battered woman and a tortured soul.

In her self-evaluation, she nearly hit a dark form sprawled out on the road in the far-left lane. Lexi honked to notify her companion that she had to cut into the third lane to skirt the object. "What the hell was that?"

The receding shape had the contours of an outstretched body. *Nooo. It's trash.* Lexi went to look again. The object was out of viewing range. *It was trash,* she told herself with a sudden urge to adjust her seating position.

The weather left no time to dwell on a potential body on the highway or ugly-faced men left to unknown fate behind them in the fog. The miles remaining to a place of development was paramount, and it was crucial for Lexi to focus on getting there in one piece. Lexi stared ahead and told herself, *You got this.* The flashes growing brighter and the loud rolling thunder argued to the contrary. Then there was the dimming sky and the occasional wind testing the Fiat's ability to resist powerful forces.

◆◆◆

For miles, things had moved along as they had prior to the run-in with the rusted truck, slow and tedious, and showered with climate uncertainty. Lexi was wondering how bad the damage was to the side of her vehicle when the smell of fire reached her nose. She detected the smoke on the lower hills to her left. It drifted inward with the fog and pounding rain. *How could a fire—* Her thought was cut short by the sight of hazy flames burning off the highway. The van was upside down, blazing a superb yellow throughout the interior. Lexi averted her eyes to preserve her sanity. She did not want to see a burning corpse. It was too much. In her mind flashed the bloody arm hanging out the window at the last crash site, and the possible body she'd seen lying in the road, followed by ugly faces. *This is the highway to Hell,* she thought, rolling along at a slower speed to avoid whatever caused the van to flip over and clear the guard railing.

There could be survivors. Lexi fought her cowardice and gave cursory glances to the eastern hills around the van. She pictured hairless, black and red charred figures with the fat of their flesh still sizzling. They were reaching for her, begging for the burning to stop from drooping lips melted in some places to the bone. *I can't take it. I can't take it.* Lexi's mind washed away the blistering phantoms into a crying wind. From what she could truly see, the hills were lifeless. *Call 911.* She went to retrieve her phone without looking down and determined her companion's passenger was in a better position to do so. She resolved to put the fiery scene behind her, plenty fine with assuming that her companion would indeed make the call.

NINE

Lexi twitched with an involuntary spasm. In her eyes was a glimmer of hope. They'd reached the limit of the canyon, and with it went the fog and oppressive wind trapped between the hills. The vista opened up into farmland, and Lexi shed some tears of joy at the sight of a slight, yet sufficient, development to the northeast and west. While the pressing thunderous lighting storm resided on the approaching horizon, she was free of the walls that bound her sight and stole her every other breath. It was enough to let her sit back in her seat and lessen the tension in her arms.

From the canyon's exit she could see a motel, Denny's restaurant, and gas station. The three comforting sights evoked a longing smile. After observing the vacant parking lots and the unlit stillness of the building's windows, her smile sank. The people of Lebec were in hiding from the weather. Besides her companion on the road, there wasn't a soul in sight. She passed an IKEA, numerous gas stations, fast-food places, an outlet mall, and warehouses, all without the slightest activity.

Looking forward with widening eyes, Lexi had forgotten a huge bump in the road, the I-99 north interchange heading to Bakersfield and Fresno. She shot up in her seat, watching her companion for an indication of a lane change. Lexi turned on the back wipers for an improved view. She knew she would have to follow wherever it was her companion went, and it put her teeth on edge. "Stick to the right," Lexi pleaded.

The interchange parted. Lexi bit down on her lower lip, threatening to split the paling pigment. Her bottled inner pleas were granted, and her companion stayed right. Lexi rocked forward three times, shouting in a low volume, "Yes! Yes! Yes! You're gonna make it." Her hands rubbed the steering wheel, feeling her palms burn from the friction. Lexi could smell the stress sweat on her hands. It smelt like old tires. She was desperate to wash them clean, and herself for that matter.

In making the transition onto the I-5 north to San Francisco and Sacramento, the sky darkened, and the rain turned into hail. The weather thrashed the Fiat's windshield with an onslaught of icy pellets. Lexi was afraid the chunks of ice were capable of breaking the glass. They sounded like a flock of birds all pecking in unison to get in. She eyeballed the thunderclouds to the west, closing in. The radiant zigzagging flashes of solid white sliced down the deep teal draped across the hills and lowland. Rumbles capable of rocking the intestines were unleashed, trembling Lexi at her core.

Her companion drew up from the rear to Lexi's right-side window and hailed her with a honk. The passenger, an alarmed young Hispanic female, was holding up a piece of paper beside her equally alarmed mother. It read, "Urgent, call us" and provided a phone number below. Lexi nodded and felt for her phone, not losing sight of the two-lane highway. With great care, she brought the phone's screen above her steering wheel.

Her eyes bugged at the twenty-six missed calls. "What the fuck? How the fuck did I silence my phone? God dammit." Lexi choked the device like it had a neck she could snap. Her paroxysm was abrupt to cease when reason reminded her she was being watched. Her thumb clicked the silent switch back to off. She glanced at her companions. Their spooked demeanor read they'd witnessed her momentary meltdown.

Lexi tried to dial the number and pressed a five instead of a six. She tried again and pressed a two instead of a one. Taking a short breather to collect herself, she attempted a third time. Her thumb was not cooperating; the shakes in it were too jumpy. In a fourth attempt, Lexi was developing a noticeable twitch in her right eye, making it twice as hard to dial in the right sequence. She was also having issues focusing between the phone's screen and the frequent looks out the windshield. *Relax,* she whined in her head, on the verge of tears.

"Let the punishment fit the crime!"

The jarring high notes of the ringtone sent the phone falling to the floor. "Nooowa!"

The underground rumblings shook the name "Mom" on the phone's screen. Lexi had somehow answered the call. Holding the steering wheel as straight as possible, she went to grab the device and managed to swat it under the seat in her haste.

"Son of a bitch! This isn't happening."

Lexi cast a look at her companions to

communicate what she'd done. Their expressions of dilated shock said they already knew. "We have to stop! I have to pull over and get my phone!"

The passenger in the brown car cuffed her ear and shook her head, saying what Lexi believed to be "I can't hear you." Lexi repeated herself. Her companions faced each other in serious conversation.

Lighting struck near the Fiat, causing Lexi to shrug in surprise. She looked out the windshield. The hail was no more; it was back to rain, a treacherous downpour. She heard her mom hollering indistinguishable words.

"Mom, I can't hear you! I dropped my phone!"

The Fiat's steering wheel wrenched from a patch of collected water on the highway. Lexi drew in earnest over the wheel, fixing her car's alignment. In her peripheral vision, she could see her companions raise another sheet of white paper. She glanced over twice to read the message: "We have to get off on Taft Highway exit." The passenger pointed forward. Lexi frowned, wondering why, and signaled okay. *Get the phone then.* Lexi swallowed; her mouth was so dry. She heard her mom continuing to talk. "Mom, I can't hear you! I dropped my phone! I will call you when I get off the freeway!"

Lexi exhaled her frustration as the brown car took the lead, staying in the second lane. She glimpsed a green road sign ahead. San Francisco was still 296 miles away.

TEN

Red taillights appeared ahead in Lexi's lane. From the madness of the elements, the vehicle appeared to be stalled. She eased over the flooded road into her companion's lane, providing them with two car lengths for safety between vehicles. It was then the red taillights began to appear to move backwards. *Oh, shit.* They *were* moving backwards and at a reckless pace. The red dots shot down the highway as two demonic eyes. "Watch out!" Lexi shouted to her companion's car.

At the speed the reckless vehicle was moving, she fully expected to see it fly off the road. Then something frightening beyond measure occurred, and the vehicle swerved in and out of both lanes. Lexi's eyes went wide. Her companion hit their brakes to avoid hitting the backwards car while Lexi shot into the left lane, feeling her wheels lose grip for a moment. She huffed with panic, watching the erratic car collide with her companions. In a second of self-preservation, Lexi pushed the gas to gain the speed necessary to avoid a collision. The car went at her bumper first and she swerved off the road, kicking up water in a near miss.

A vivid white permeated the Fiat, absorbing the world out of existence in a powerful glow. Lexi gasped as she looked away, somehow maintaining her tires on the road. She squeezed her eyelids shut, but they did not keep out the piercing light. The life of the blinding flash was fleeting but felt eternal. Once it was over, a loud boom came down from overhead, a sound resembling a jumbo jet landing in a nosedive atop the Fiat's roof. Lexi screamed. The ground was rumbling with a rabid furry, dazing her senses. In the flurry of confusion, it was near impossible to navigate a single lane. Lexi's hands clung to the steering wheel, her eyes plagued by photo-bleached spots. Past the ringing in her ears, she could hear her mother hollering from beneath her seat.

When the lurid quaking ebbed and the Fiat was back under manageable control, Lexi checked on her companions. Behind her was a black sports car about to collide with her rear end. Lexi downed the accelerator. In a quick maneuver, the sports car pulled into the left lane and sped up parallel to the Fiat. "Mom, call the police!" Lexi shouted, half out of her head with fright. The sports car teased ramming her from the side in a constant sweeping back and forth motion. "Stop! Why are you doing this? Stop it!" Lexi cried, bracing for a hit.

A blue contorted face was pressed against the passenger side window of the black car. It was staring at Lexi with protruding bloodshot eyes. The man's tongue was out, licking the window with every antagonizing sweep of the vehicle. Lexi was already gunning the Fiat at an unforgiving speed, and there was no faster she could push the machine. She got the urge to ram the sports car in a last desperate act, realizing she was going to pass out at the wheel because her ever increasing shakes and heart rate assured it.

Feeling her convulsing arms start to give way on the controls, Lexi screamed until her voice cracked. She was going out. *I have to find an exit! Give me an exit!* At the speed she was moving, her windshield was obscured by rain. The only way to get a view of the outside was to look out the side windows. In one of her many shifting glances at the black car's threats to launch into her, she made a discovery. The ugly-faced man in the passenger seat was thrown against the window in a lurch at her. His eyes nearly came out of their sockets when he hit the glass, his nose bent up like a pig's and his tongue lolled at the corner of his uneven mouth. It was like he was a doll switched on by the momentum of the car.

Lexi's face contracted in a whine, for she gathered that the man was dead. At that instant, a terror transcending thought peered from behind the body with a psychopath's smile. *The driver.* Lexi twitched from the shock of the man's deranged face. Her brain did not want to accept the clown as reality. It took a dangerous stare to prove the clown-faced terror was indeed real. Lexi screamed and didn't stop despite the cracking in her voice. The clown pushed the dead passenger over into the dashboard for a better look at his intended victim. His black arched eyebrows drew down over a streaked white painted face and his red erected lips, which radiated the highest form of grotesque desire.

The petrifying sight sucked the air out of Lexi's lungs. In a state of sheer panic, Lexi crushed the gas pedal underfoot at an already lethal speed. She gasped, swatting the car horn as if it had the power to open her airways and find help. She found herself tangled in her seat belt, attempting an escape so she could run away to nowhere, all while making rapid sounds of a gagging hiccup. This was it, and she knew it, as she rose out of her seat in a final plea for the thinnest straw hole of oxygen. As the blurring darkness of tunnel vision crept over her eyes and the overactive veins in her forehead, neck, and throat protruded, she gave the laughing clown a funny face of her own. The funniest she had ever made.

The clown's laughing paused. The Fiat was thrown into the sports car at full blast. Lexi was half unconscious and giving herself over to death when her eyes closed on the scene of the sports car fishtailing off the road into a barbed wire fence and herself driving off into farmland.

White light flashed behind the curtains of Lexi's eyelids. In the flashes jumped a smiling clown out of her memory. Lexi sat up with a start to the ground vibrating the Fiat. Out of reflex, she gripped the steering wheel to get her aching head to cease swirling. In swings of distorted observation, she whined at the pouring windows. She struggled to get out of her seat and forgot she was buckled down. Lexi unhooked herself, spinning from view to view with a renewed panic. Her companions were gone, and she couldn't tell what direction the highway was. She saw the black car in the distance out her rear, left-side window. The fear of finding herself in the middle of open land trumped her fear of the clown. All she could think was, *I have to get out of here.*

Trembling on the verge of collapse, she tried to start the engine. The Fiat wouldn't turn over. "No! No!" Lexi repeated, pummeling the steering wheel with her fists. "Start! God damn you! Start!" Lexi felt her breaths shrinking. "Ahhh!" She opened the door, and the rain soaked her in a manner of seconds. She ducked under her seat, dipping her knees into the flooded mud in search of her cell phone. "C'mon! Where the fuck is it?" Her hand searched the compact space, her fingertips tapping a hard object. Lexi snagged the device. Standing up, she had to shake off a momentary dizzy spell that left her leaning on the car for stability. She smacked the clinging hair in her vision and did a wild search for any signs of development.

The faintest image of a building appeared behind the black sports car at the limit of her sight. It appeared to have a towering sign separate from the main building, indicative of a gas station. Lexi grunted, pinching her features as though she might cry because she had to get past the psycho's vehicle in order to avoid a serious detour that her failing breath would not allow. The danger reminded her to snatch her purse off the passenger seat to bring her blue pepper spray along.

In a hasty trudge through the mud, Lexi's eyes stalked the black car. She kept what distance she could from the vehicle while over and over in her head, the clown got out of the car and took chase after her. She knew if the clown did take chase, odds were she would not have the air supply to outrun the monster. Lexi was a super-fast runner, and under normal circumstances the clown wouldn't have had the slimmest chance in catching her. It was out here in the sticky muck of farmland and its showering climate, adding pounds to her clothes, where she didn't have much of a chance.

Lexi could see the puffy red hair of the clown slumped over in the driver's seat. With pepper spray in her hand and her phone in the other, she fought for control over her insufficient breaths. Her negative thoughts switched gears and told her the sports car would, at any moment, turn on and run her down. With several looks over her shoulder, the car taunted her with that potential outcome. Lexi saw herself fleeing for her life as the vehicle mowed her down. The thought concluded with the clown laughing as her head came apart under a wheel. Lexi's face opened up with a want to scream, and she demanded her brain to suppress the oxygen expenditure she could not spare.

Just then, she did hear a car, only it was not a car; it was a truck and far off for someone on their feet. The vehicle was driving north on the I-5.

"Hey!" Lexi shouted, waving her arms.

The truck drove on.

"Hey!" she yelled with all her might.

A lightning bolt struck down and flashed the truck out of sight. When it returned to view, the truck was on a shoulder road, apparent by its deviation from an overpass.

Lexi was out of air, her expression twisted in pure mental anguish. The truck disappeared behind the building she was forced to run full tilt for. The ground quaked. Lexi was not fazed by her vision rattling, nor her unequal footing. She was on auto pilot, and it was "run until you pass out" time. She would either make it or not. Pressing the gas on her legs, she made gasping pleas for a new level of speed. The rain seemed to be pushing her in reverse.

Stiffening at the knees, a hopeful sight gave her a rush of confidence. Through the rain spraying into her eyes, she could see the towering sign's logo evolve out of the gloom. It was a gas station and mini mart. Lexi's mind switched gears to a positive thought. *I can make it.* She swung a look over her shoulder. The black sports car had not budged. *I can make it.*

With determination and grit, she swung her arms at full extension to quicken the stride of her impeded lower half. Her mouth was flushed with water with each struggling huff of air. The sports car was receding into the storm. Keeping her ears open for the clown's engine, her focus shifted strictly to the back side of the market. She put her pace into a dangerous overdrive, a pace that was oxygen intensive. Panting in narrow sips of air, she gained on her goal. The building grew closer and closer.

Lexi hopped a barbed wire fence, finding herself six feet from the I-5 south. The traction of the pavement beneath the water gave her a boost in stride. She was crossing the land between the two highways when a lightning bolt flashed to her left. The boost she received in stride on the I-5 north made the quaking ground easier to manage. Hopping another barbed wire fence, she was a hundred yards from the market.

Her body was on fumes. Lexi had to stop to rest on her knees and fight for breath. Her heart was beating so hard it hurt to think. Soaked to the bone, she was beginning to feel a deep freeze kick in. She held her cramping sides and raised in a slight jog. Despite the rain shooting into her mouth, her throat couldn't have been drier. She licked her lips, breathing out of her mouth only. Her lips stung and her nose was plugged tight.

In her vulnerable position, she gave a look back in the clown's direction. The sight froze her heart in place. In the premature twilight, there was the silhouette of a person dressed in baggy clown attire with wide hair standing beside the sports car, watching her. The whites of her eyes exploded with a whispered whine. Lexi turned and pressed on with what strength she could muster. In glances of sheer panic, she observed the clown do nothing other than watch her.

Lexi tripped and picked herself up, clawing into the mud to gain her footing. Pushing off, she strained each muscle to the max to keep moving. It was one foot in front of the other. The weather wanted her to give up, hitting her with wave after wave of freezing sheets of rain. Lexi was too far into flight mode to contemplate anything other than running for survival. She would tax every ounce of strength she had to make it to the back side of the market.

When she did reach the building, she fell against the structure to hold herself up. Drenched and dripping, she inched her way towards the front entrance on juddering legs. A blurry figure opened the door for her, and she collapsed in sturdy arms, saying in an oxygen deprived voice, "Please... help me. He's—" Lexi was cut off. She had passed out.

ELEVEN

Lexi heard a light buzzing sound in the darkness. Her eyes came apart in blinks. When her vision cleared, she discovered the source of the noise was a Presto heat dish pointed at her. She lifted with a quick look around and found herself wrapped in an electric blanket on the storeroom floor. Two men talking in low voices at the front of the mini mart stole her gaze. She touched her crotch and breasts to verify her clothes had not been removed or tampered with. Her sweater and pants were soggy to the touch, and she did not like the sensation movement produced. To her relief, her private areas showed no signs of violation.

The men were scrutinizing the parking lot and gas pumps with considerable unease. She was eager to tell them about the clown but was not in the frame of mind to push her swollen vocal cords, much less articulate the situation to be of any benefit to anyone. One of the men was an older Indian gentleman and an employee of the store. The other was a taller, considerably stronger Caucasian male in his mid to late twenties.

During her observation of the men, the dim world outside flashed in the store windows and then rumbled the floor. Lexi shivered, pulling her heated blanket higher and hugging herself. She wondered if she could talk in a whole sentence. The phlegm was so thick and her throat hole so tight she was doubtful. Still, she had to try. Her mouth opened and a single harsh word rasped out. "Water." The men did not hear her and went on conversing. An ineffectual moan matched the sadness developing on Lexi's tensed features. She took in several preparatory breaths to speak. Then, it dawned on her. *My phone? My purse?* She lifted the blanket, also scanning her immediate surroundings. Her eyes hung open in thought. She cupped her mouth and looked at the back of the store, letting out an involuntary whimper. She had dropped her only items of recourse en route.

The men heard Lexi's suffering and came rushing over. Her hair bristled at their encroachment upon her personal space. The younger white male sat on his haunches and put a weighty hand on her shoulder. "Are you injured?"

Lexi flexed downward from the neck and thought twice about pulling away, afraid the act would advertise her defenseless position and bestir a wanton free-for-all. Maintaining her composure, she shook her head no.

The young man leaned back and removed his hand from her shoulder, putting Lexi's horripilation into a state of gradual easing.

"What has happened to you?" asked the store clerk with a deep accent. His tired eyes peered into Lexi's with convincing concern.

With the slightest audible pitch, she said, "There's... can I get a water, first?"

"Yes." The clerk hastened to her request.

Lexi noticed the younger man watched the clerk instead of her. His nervous body language was not signature of a lecherous opportunist. She also couldn't help noticing that he was quite handsome. He had flowing dark brown hair, darker brown eyes, and smooth features with a thin layer of facial scruff. He reminded her of a young Mickey Rourke.

The clerk returned, handing Lexi a bottle of Aquafina. She downed the liquid in one continuous chug. The hydration cooled her insides like peppermint candy. Pulling the empty bottle from her lips, she released a quenched exhale.

"A man dressed as a clown tried to run me off the road. He chased me here. Me and..." Lexi stared inward, thinking of her lost companion's fate. The men exchanged a brief look of heightened apprehension. Without lifting her eyes, she went on. "There was a dead man in the passenger seat of his car. I think he killed him." Lexi swallowed and the saliva traveling down her sore throat was loud in her ears. She swung a look up at the two men, exclaiming in terror, "Lock the doors."

Without delay, the clerk raced into his glass-encased cubicle, set behind shelves of flavored treats, energy shots, erection pills, and roses. The younger man pulled a phone from his pocket and made his way back to the front of the store to look out the windows. The clerk joined him, spinning the keys he retrieved from under the cash register into the door's lock.

"What's he driving?" asked the young man with an antsy look back.

Lexi coughed to be heard. "A black muscle car."

"You know the make?"

Lexi shook her head.

Putting the phone to his ear, the young man peered out the windows. "I don't see anything. You?" he asked the clerk.

The clerk's voice was shaky. "No, my friend."

"He was—" Lexi was interrupted by the younger man raising his hand for quiet.

The two listened in on the call.

"I want to report a murder... yes... Nick Turner... apparently, a man wearing a clown outfit, driving a black muscle car of unknown make, chased a woman into the Fuel 'n Snack off Highway 119. The woman said he has the murder victim in the car with him." He looked at Lexi for verification, and she nodded. "Yes, she's with us... no... three of us." The young man glanced at the ceiling lights. "So far." Lexi's breath labored at the likelihood of the storm knocking out the electricity. It gave her an urgency to pee. "Okay... and do you know how long that will take?... Okay... no, I don't see him anywhere." He peered out the windows. "We are... yes, yes... I understand. No, I mean, what can you do? You know." He shrugged. "How long do you think it'll take to clear up?... *Really*... okay." He cast his eyes at the others in the room to share the lousy news. Lexi's head tilted with a lip-parted frown. "No, she's not injured... yeah, you want to talk to her?" The young man headed over to Lexi. "She wants to talk to you."

Lexi took the phone after asking the clerk for another water.

"This is Lexi." Her voice sounded gravelly.

"Hi, Lexi. I need you to tell me exactly what happened to you."

"Let me take a sip of water. My throat's dry."

The clerk handed her a bottle.

"Take your time."

Lexi's throat felt like someone was pinching it at the base after she swallowed. "I was driving on the I-5 north alongside another vehicle when a black car came at us in reverse." The operator began typing. "The man in the sports car tried to run me and the other driver off the road... I don't know what happened to the other driver and her daughter. He hit her, and lightning struck, and we got separated." Lexi coughed, feeling the phlegm in her throat jump. "Sorry."

"You're fine."

"He tried to rear-end me. I sped up, and he went to the left side of my car. That's when I saw the dead man in the front seat and that the driver was wearing clown makeup." The memory of the clown's deranged face gave Lexi goosebumps.

"Are you positive the passenger was dead?"

"Yes. He was pressed against the window, not moving."

"Then what happened?"

"The driver was teasing to hit my car from the side. He kept weaving in and out of my lane at the last second. I didn't know what to do, so I ramm…" Lexi's voice box dried out and she had to take another sip. "Rammed his car and we went off the road." Lexi omitted the part of her passing out at the wheel to avoid showing a sign of weakness in front of the men. "I got out of my car and ran here. The clown got out of his car too but was too slow to catch me."

The men looked out the flashing windows.

"Well, Lexi, like I was telling Nick, we'll have a unit out to you as soon as we can."

"How long are you thinking it'll take?" The rumbling in the floor caused Lexi to squirm.

"It's tough to say. The highway's a mess. The roads are flooded from Copus Road on. In the meantime, I want you to stay together and alert and call us back if you see anything out of the ordinary. Especially if you see this clown character."

Lexi put a cold hand to her throbbing head.

"You can count on it."

"Also, do you have the make of the vehicle you were beside that was hit?"

"No. It was a brown car. Four door."

"Brown, four door. Excellent. Lexi, can I talk to the supervisor on duty?"

"Yeah."

Lexi held the phone out for the clerk. "She, wants to talk to you."

The man rubbed his hands on his navy-blue Dickies to take the phone. "This is Bhavin... yes, the doors are locked... I have, yes, very secure... Is no problem. Yes... ah, truly... is good, thank you madame, much appreciated your services. Goodbye." Bhavin handed Nick his phone back and waved his long index finger at the two. "I have a battery-operated light in the storage closet. I will get it."

"Good idea," Nick said.

Bhavin sidestepped Lexi and disappeared behind the door between his glass cubical and the cooler section where the overstock was kept.

When Lexi looked back at Nick, their eyes met in a short unintentional stare. Nick glanced outside and back at Lexi. "I never got your name?"

"It's Lexi."

Nick looked down, then outside. "I hate to

admit it, but I have a major phobia of clowns. My brother showed me that film, *Poltergeist,* when I was five, with the clown that pulls the kid under the bed. Have you seen it?"

Lexi nodded.

"That picture ruined me. For years my brother would put these creepy clown dolls in my bed at night. Scared me half to death, the prick." Nick glanced at Lexi and laughed at himself while looking down.

Lexi smiled and tossed her damp hair back with her hand. She was not used to a man of his strapping and attractive quality being so unguarded and shy. It was a huge turn-on. She imagined him holding her as Chad did Rachael but was brought out of her fantasy by Bhavin stepping around her. In the clerk's hand was an orange and black lantern in the shape of a flashlight. Its powerful size was a reassuring sight.

"Have you tested the light?" Lexi asked.

"Smart," the clerk said, clicking the light on and off.

Lexi huffed under her breath at the negligence. "Nick, can I use your phone?" Lexi knew her parents must be worried sick.

"Yeah." Walking over, he pressed in the code

to unlock the keypad.

"Thanks."

"Anytime."

The two smiled at each other for a prolonged period. Lexi broke the spell, taking a drink of water. She stood, her luminous blue eyes avoiding him. She headed to the opposite side of the store. The annoying soggy cling of her clothes distracted her secret glances over the racks at Nick. She settled in the corner of the cooler section. The phone rang, but nobody answered. Lexi checked the number for accuracy and dialed again. No answer. *What the fuck, Mom. I asked you to be by the phone.* Lightning flashed over the Pringles and Lay's potato chips. Lexi waited for the rumbling to stop and dialed her parents a third time. There was no answer. She clenched her teeth and shook the phone, giving her a splitting headache. *You can't trust anybody.*

After her tantrum settled down, the pounding in her skull lessened, letting Lexi reason that her parents had never failed to be by their phone. She contemplated her dad having had a heart attack or stroke, or her mom, and cussed at herself for not having their cell phone numbers memorized. *I have to get home. How am I going to get out of here without my purse? I have to call the rental company. They'll send a tow truck.* Lexi envisioned a greasy, ugly-faced tow truck driver taking her to a secluded shop. *I have to get home!* Lexi clutched her mouth, shaking like she had thought it out loud. She peered over the potato chips at Nick and Bhavin, thinking she had. The two were talking at the entrance windows. Lexi bent forward, cringing, holding her mouth so she wouldn't cry. *I could ask Nick for a lift home. Call the rental company. They'll pick up the car, and Mom and Dad can spot the money for Nick's troubles. Yeah. It'd be nice to get to know him better on the trip over.* Lexi lifted to admire Nick. *Yeah. It'll work. Assuming he says yes. He seems like he would,* Lexi thought as she watched him.

The store lights flickered, and Lexi's legs took on a life of their own, moving toward her companions.

"Nick, thanks for letting me use your phone."

"No worries." Nick pocketed the device, staying vigilant on the property with Bhavin.

A heavy wind whistled in the slits of the convenience store doors, pushing on them to open. In unison, the lights flickered, and the three raised their heads to the ceiling.

"We're definitely losing these lights," Nick

said.

"I agree," added Bhavin.

"Do you have any other flashlights?" asked Lexi.

"I do not, no."

"You can use my cell's flashlight, Lexi."

She smiled at Nick, rotating at the hips a bit, too engrossed by her building fascination to let the cling of her clothing bother her. "You're sweet; thank you." *Wait for the right time to ask him.*

Lexi drew to the window adjacent to Nick's, standing at arm's length with a want for his arms to be around her. The evening was on the brink of nightfall. The clouds carpeted the sky with a factory's soot as rain poured over the edges of the gas station's canopy, cascading in a rectangular waterfall. Lexi scanned the darkest corners for the faintest semblance of the clown. In her search, she came across something almost as unnerving. She looked at Nick with puzzled shock stamped on her features. *You want him to be who he's not.* Lexi looked out at the parking lot, proving to herself that her eyes did not deceive her. The lifted Toyota Ram could not be denied. Her eyes twitched on the license plate, reading, "My Beast."

TWELVE

Lexi went back to her heated section of the store. There she stood, hugging herself with one arm and biting the skin at the edges of her fingernails. She was watching Nick from behind, wondering how it was he did not recognize her. *Or did he?* Her eyes narrowed at him. *He's playing you to get in your pants.* In her experience, that was fair speculation. She recalled how he'd laughed at her on the highway when he stopped short.

Lexi glared, wanting to walk up and slap him in the face. She heard her therapist's words, *Our bodies are by invitation only.* Lexi bit her lower lip, considering letting him have a go at her for a ride home, if that was the actual price and not just in her head. *Why's he have to be so fucking hot? It's not right. It was a brief interaction, and I did antagonize him with the horn. He flipped me off. I antagonized him, though. I'm making excuses for him. How many times can I play the sucker?* Lexi huffed. *Fuck! How am I going to get home? I have to get home.*

She became conscious of Bhavin observing her stare at Nick and pulled her finger out of her mouth. The clerk was prompt to redirect his attention outside. Lexi, embarrassed at getting caught, redirected her attention to the items on the store shelves. Her impromptu browsing led her to a traveler's nail kit, inside of which contained a sharp pair of mini scissors she could set between her middle fingers and stab with in a pinch.

Lexi scoped out the store for security cameras, finding several built into the ceiling tiles. The place was covered from every angle.

When lightning strikes, don't hesitate.

"Lexi, where'd you leave your car at?"

"Huh?" Nick's question pulled her out of her head.

"Where'd you leave your car at?"

Lexi got down on her knees on the electric blanket and extended her hands to the heat dish. It was an excuse to stay put. "It's..." She began to signal to the vehicle's actual location but got suspect of the question. She did not want to let the men know her car was out of reach. "...behind the store. In the field."

"Shit, he was that close?"

"Yeah." Lexi swallowed.

Nick looked at Bhavin with alarm. "There's no back door he can get into, right?"

"I have a delivery door, and it's padlocked across the bottom three times." Bhavin raised three fingers to Nick and Lexi. "Three. We are secure. We also have my post. Very secure. He will most certainly not get in." Bhavin gestured at the glass-encased compartment housing the register. "It is bulletproof."

Lexi eyed the fortified cubicle. A thought entered her mind. "Bhavin, do you have a gun?"

"That I do not have, no. I do not condone violence of any kind. God will protect us, I have prayed. Do not worry, my friends. We are protected and blessed under the Almighty."

There is no God. Two men with ugly faces strolled into Lexi's memory. Their countenances pressed over her prepubescent body with salacious ambition. The little girl was paralyzed. She pretended she was receiving shots from the doctor to endure the excruciating pain. Her small hands pressed her jacket to her ears to tune out the thrusting grunts and cheers.

Lexi snapped her teeth and whipped her head to the side to return to the present. She turned to the heater to avoid making a remark she would regret to Bhavin about his God. The two men were back to surveying the wall of windows. Lexi took the opportunity to eye the nail kit. She knew lightning was coming soon, but lightning was not what she was treated to. The store's lights went out, following a mean upswing of wind. With a gasp, Lexi went erect in the pitch black, her heart pounding out of her chest.

Bhavin illuminated the store with a beam of light that cast animated shadows in every direction.

"Welp, this sucks," said Nick.

"Yes," Bhavin agreed.

Evening out her breath, it occurred to Lexi that the cameras were off and that her section was especially low lit. Nick and Bhavin were busy in conversation, so now was her chance. She eased over to the shelf and slipped the nail kit quietly off the rack. She was partway to her blanket where she intended to conceal the item when the lights came back on. As a distraction, Lexi fell onto the blanket, landing on her shoulder with her back to the men, stuffing the kit out of sight.

She rolled over and saw that the men were observing her.

"Are you okay?" Nick asked.

Lexi wasn't sure if either had caught the theft. She rubbed her wrist, which was injured during the fake fall. "Yeah, I lost my balance."

"Would you like some ice?" Bhavin asked, revealing he'd not seen the crime.

"No, I'm good." She wanted to ask for another water and to use the restroom. *Later.* "Thank you, though. I think I'll take a rest."

Lexi climbed under the blanket, facing the heater. She proceeded to blindly open the nail kit and remove the scissors without damaging the box to reseal it. Placing the scissors in her pocket, she waited for her opportunity to put the box back on the shelf.

Her opportunity came swiftly. The lightning made a grand reappearance above the store, blazing the interior with potent white flashes that stole the electricity in a quaking wake.

Unknown minutes passed in the shadowy store. In the intervening span, Lexi devised a plan to get Nick's truck and make him come with her to her folks' place with no strings attached. The plan was simple: she would—

"Lexi!" Nick exclaimed with equal caution and excitement.

She moved promptly to the window, hooked to the glass like the others.

"You think it is the police?" Bhavin asked.

"Hard to tell," Nick responded, straining his eyes.

"I would not want to patrol tonight. I can tell you that."

"I hear ya. I haven't seen a storm this bad in... gosh, I can't even tell you."

"Bhavin, get ready with the keys to your office," Lexi said, watching the two approaching headlights out in the black showering distance.

"I am prepared."

The three stood rapt, in silence. The volume of the rain and wind was amplified with the lack of competing sound, where seconds became hours and minutes, insufferable durations.

"It's him, it's the clown," Lexi cried, her face rearranging. "Look!"

THIRTEEN

Bhavin held the unsteady light on the floor next to Lexi, shading her features in a creepy, fright-filled glow. The whites of her eyes read that she was in a state of shock, and it was possible that she might attack them by mistake, when in actuality, it was just her funny face making an appearance.

Nick raised a hand. "Lexi, it's a truck."

She jabbed the scissors between her fingers at Nick and the big rig. "He probably switched vehicles."

Nick gestured for calm. "Okay, well, let's see who comes out of the truck."

"He could ram the store." She peered out the window, trembling. "Bhavin, turn off the light,"

Lexi demanded.

The store was thrown into darkness.

"Lexi, let's remain calm."

"What do we do if it's him?"

"Uh…"

"God will protect us."

"Oh, shut up the fuck up about God! God isn't looking after us. If you haven't noticed, Bhavin, the world's a pretty fucked-up place. Take a look around once in a while. Does it look like a divine presence gives a shit about us? No, it doesn't, does it? Providence is bullshit—it's nonsense. We're fucked and then we die. And that's the reality of things. Accept it. Stop living in fantasyland."

A heavy stillness dropped over the store, broken by the big rig pulling into the gas station. The sound of uncontrollable sobbing was heard. "I'm sorry," Lexi whined. "I didn't mean to—"

"It is okay. I do not take offense. I, too, struggle with having faith."

The squeal of the big rig coming to a complete stop put an urgency in Nick's voice. "If he doesn't see anyone inside, he should leave, so, let's hide."

Feeling her way to the closest rack, Lexi crouched down. She heard the others pick a different aisle, bringing a quiver to her lips. *They don't want to be near me anymore.* She swallowed with a want to cry out in pain. She could hear them whispering. *They're talking about me.*

The air grew breathless with the sound of the truck's driver's side door closing. Lexi dried her eyes, scrutinizing the bulky figure crossing the headlights. Wading footfalls splashed to the front entrance, clomping on to the sheltered entryway. The doors were jerked on, and the figure bumped the glass for a look inside. A cell phone light pierced the glass, sending Lexi into the crinkling bags at her back. "Shit," she whispered, leaning forward, balancing on a single hand and stiffening the sweaty grip on her scissors as the light scanned the interior.

Lightning flashed, followed by rumbling thunder.

"Grandpa!" The scream was a child's.

"Open the door!" Lexi yelled, running to the entrance. Nick and Bhavin were on her heels. The bearded older man framed in the window was startled at the mad rush and stumbled back.

"Grandpa!"

Lexi saw the crown of the little girl's head in the truck. "We're coming."

Bhavin struggled to steady the keys into the

lock while Nick held the flashlight for him.

C'mon! Lexi thought, visualizing taking the keys from the clerk to do it herself.

The doors came apart with an aggressive wind. Lexi ran out to the limit of the shelter, prepared to brave the rain, but thought better of it, for the little girl was in the arms of her grandfather and almost to her. And she couldn't very well offer to comfort the child in soaked clothing. As it was, there was nothing she could do to dry out her undergarments and the damp and cold imprints they gave her pants and dress shirt.

"Phew. I was beginning to think we had been misdirected," said the bearded man, pushing off his hood.

"We lost electricity," Lexi said, following the two into the store.

"It's out throughout most of the county." The older man looked at Nick and Bhavin, who were holding the doors open for them and said, "Hello."

Bhavin locked the doors behind them, leaving the wind moaning to get in. Nick gave the clerk back his light.

The little girl's pink hood opening was pressed into the side of her grandfather's hip. Lexi knelt beside her and asked the older man in a soft voice,

"What's her name?"

"Candice."

"What a pretty name."

Lexi went to rub the precious angel's back when the scissors gleamed in the light. Lexi about broke her fingers yanking the sharp object off to conceal it in her pocket. She glanced at the grandfather to gauge whether or not he'd seen the weapon. His countenance was too indistinct to tell. She decided it didn't matter and rubbed the girl's back.

"It's alright, Candice. You're safe."

The girl squeezed into her grandfather's hip, and Lexi's head tilted with a pensive smile.

"She doesn't like the lightning."

"Nobody does," Lexi said, getting closer to Candice. The girl peeked at Lexi and Lexi whispered, "Hi there."

Candice shied away, looking up at her grandfather, and tugged on his jacket. "Grandpa, when are the lights coming back on?"

"Remember what the officer said? They're working on fixing the lines."

"You spoke to the police?" asked Nick.

"I did. They're detouring everyone off the freeway due to the roads and highway being washed out. We were advised to stay put at this location and ride out the storm. Supposed to pass through by 4:00 A.M. They'll be sending an officer to let us know when it's permissible to leave."

"4:00 A.M.?" Lexi asked, disguising her worry for the little girl.

"That's what the officer said."

Lexi put on a smile and brushed hair out of the little girl's eyes. She poked her cute button nose and whispered at a volume the other adults couldn't hear. "I'll be right back." Lexi stood. "Nick, can I use your phone again? I want to update my parents."

"Yeah."

Nick unlocked his cell, and Lexi took the device, retreating into the back of the store where it was unlit.

The phone did not complete a full ring.

"Lexi?" Her mother's tone was frantic.

"Mom, where have you been?"

"Lexi, I can't hear you."

Lexi eased her grip on the phone. "Mom, I can't talk loud."

"Is it her?" hollered her father in the background.

"Yes, Ron, quiet, I can't hear her. Lexi—"

"Mom, I can't talk loud. Can you hear me?"

"Barely. Where have you been? I've been calling you for hours."

"What do you mean? I called you several times and you didn't pick up."

"What! We didn't receive a call."

Lexi's forehead tensed. "Well, I called you and you didn't pick up."

Her father was saying something Lexi couldn't make out.

"Yes, Ron, alright. I'm trying to listen."

"Lexi, I don't know what to tell you. We've been by the phone. We were about to call the police. Where are you?"

"I'm at the Fuel 'n Snack off Highway 119 in Bakersfield."

"She's in Bakersfield. Are you okay?"

"Yes, I'm fine. The police are having us wait the storm out because of the flooding."

"You're okay, though?"

"Yes. I will explain everything when I get home."

"She's okay. Lexi, I..." There was muffled talk between her parents.

"What, Mom?"

"Lexi, we're having Drew, Phil, and Lisa pick

you up. They'll meet you at the Fuel 'n Snack first thing in the morning."

"Mom, no. I have a ride home."

"Lexi, we do not want you driving home alone. We have our reasons, so don't argue."

"But I'm not driving home alone." Lexi lowered her voice. "I'm driving home with Candice and her grandfather."

"Who is that?"

"A couple of friends I've made waiting around."

"No, Lexi. Drew, Philip, and Lisa are picking you up. Now I don't want to hear another word about it."

"Mom, stop it."

"Lexi, damn it. Don't argue. We have our reasons." There were tears in her mother's voice.

"Mom, I understand you're worried."

"Let me have the phone," said Ron, irritated.

"Your father wants—"

"Lexi, Drew, Philip, and Lisa are picking you up and that's final."

"No, Dad."

"Lexi, I'm not trying to scare you, but there's a maniac loose on the five. He has already taken the lives of ten people. I do not want you to be number eleven. I want you to ride home with people I know can and will protect you." Her father's tone became sharp. "Now don't argue anymore."

Lexi tightened her arm encircling her waist, her mind resurfacing the clown and the dead man in the passenger seat, the flipped-over van on fire she'd seen, and the figure she saw on the highway that looked an awful lot like a dead person. Her attention brought Candice back into focus. She was watching the little girl the whole time.

"And, who's going to protect her?"

"Who?"

"Candice."

"Who's Candice?"

"Sorry, Dad."

"Lexi... Lexi!"

She ended the call and looked at the child. *I won't let anything happen to you. I promise.*

A strange impulse Lexi couldn't explain led her to check the call history on Nick's phone. There was no record of her earlier calls.

FOURTEEN

Lexi appeared from out of the dark, and Nick met her away from the group. She put her hand in her scissors pocket, set to strike.

"How you doin'?" he whispered, stepping into her personal space.

He's checking on me. They all check on you to get what they want. "I'm fine. I apologize for freaking out on you and Bhavin."

"No need. It's completely understandable. I'm impressed you're holding together as well as you are, considering what you've been through."

Lexi's hand withdrew from her scissors pocket. *Don't fall for it.*

"Besides, I should be apologizing to you."

"Lexi's head tilted. "For what?"

Nick cleared his throat. "I didn't mean to cut you off on the freeway. It was an accident. I didn't see you until the last minute and then it was too late."

Lexi's mouth drew open as she listened with throbbing suspense.

"I should have paid better attention. I feel terrible. It's my brother's truck. He's getting married and I was asked to drive it out to the wedding for him. As you can tell, I suck at driving it. 'The Beast,'" Nick said in a derogatory tone.

Lexi laughed some.

"I feel like such a douche bag driving around in it. You have no idea how embarrassing it is."

"I can imagine," Lexi said with another small laugh.

Nicked laughed with her. "Yeah, it's not my style, at all. And it doesn't bring out the best in people on the road, I can tell you that."

"Speaking from experience, I can see why," she said playfully.

"Yeah." Nick laughed. "Anyway, I just came over to apologize. I hope there's no hard feelings. I feel terrible about it. I would have apologized earlier, but with everything happening..."

"No, I get it. And I honked at you. It was my

fault for antagonizing the situation."

"No, it wasn't. You had every right to honk at me. I fucked up. I cut you off. And I overreacted. I acted like a complete idiot and I'm sorry."

He's perfect. "You know, it's interesting you should mention a wedding."

"Oh yeah, why's that?"

"I was stressed too. My friend was supposed to accompany me to my parents' and bailed on me last minute for preparations for her wedding."

"It appears love is in the air."

"I guess so."

A silent tension was, at an instant, between them, motioning them to converge as lovers. A building tension, which with every vibrant second of continued silence, magnified its attraction. It was that part of the movie where the man takes the woman into his arms and kisses her for the first time, when the misunderstanding of acts one, two, and three culminate in a happy ending. Lexi desired the kiss. She wanted it so badly she could taste it, but she was also afraid. Afraid it would not stop there, and she would have to drive the scissors into his stomach.

"Thanks for letting me use your phone," Lexi said, ruining the moment. She handed back the device, her hand tremors cloaked under the dim lighting.

"Again, anytime."

Lexi realized she was shaking all over from repressed passion and decided to cure her sexual energy with a subject of distraction. "My parents told me the clown has killed ten people."

"I heard."

"From who?"

"Greg." Nick thumbed toward Candice's grandfather. "Check this out."

The photo above the breaking news story put Lexi's hair on edge. It was the thin cut of his eyes, one slanted and one smaller than the other. The blank, dark penetrating stare within the uneven folds. The tilted aspect of his incongruous palsy that left his nose crooked and his mouth leaning left. The frail, light brown hair that was a far cry from the many stress grooves splitting his atavistic skull. The distinctive quality of a pedophile found in the slant of his good-natured yet predatory, gapped grin, which put him in third place for ugliest face she'd ever seen. He was a monster, Lexi concluded, even before she scrolled down to the next familiar pulse-racing photo featuring him in his clown outfit, entertaining children.

Walter Harris, age 48, was heading to a children's fundraiser for his company ESCI when he, for reasons still under investigation, ended up at his boss's estate. He broke into the home and shot and killed his boss, Tim Hughes, his wife, Carrie Hughes, two daughters, Elise and Tracy, and son Adam, after he shot and hung the family dog from a tree in the back yard. He then proceeded to cut up the bodies to dispose of on Interstate five, placing the divided remains in garbage bags.

Walter, a code writer for eight years out of Silicon Beach, divorced with two estranged daughters, was known to have bouts of unprovoked rage and homicidal tendencies. Under the care of a physician for social issues, he was recorded as a violence risk.

Dr. Dechen Maffet warned the clinic that her patient was rejecting treatment for symptoms of schizophrenia and delirium. After claiming to have recurring fantasies of killing his coworkers, Dr. Dechen was forced to reach out to Walter's employer, which may have contributed to his attack on the family. It is unknown if Walter was released from his job for his homicidal ideation toward employees and, in turn, retaliated.

Since the gruesome discovery of his

employer and family, five additional bodies in connection to the murders have been discovered on Interstate five. Walter Harris was last reported driving in Mr. Hughes's black Aston Martin, wearing a clown costume for the children's benefit he was scheduled to attend. He is believed to be somewhere in the Bakersfield area, in costume. Police are asking for your help for any tips that will aid in his arrest.

Lexi's eyes raised to Nick's, the corner of her eye monitoring Candice.

"Nuts, right?" Nick asked.

"Sure is."

"You hear of people encountering serial killers, but you don't ever expect it will happen to you."

"That's how predators operate. They surprise you." Lexi thought about how close she'd come to death and felt the cold chill from earlier on her flesh. She resisted a keen urge to rub her arms in front of Nick.

"I had this guy I grew up with named Gerald Remmer, a friend of my brother. A real oddball. I remember he wore these crazy thick black glasses like something you would see a nerd wearing in the fifties. He had a strange look about him besides the glasses, a telling something that upstairs wasn't functioning properly. Not a dangerous look, but rather a look that put you ill at ease. I asked my brother about it, and he said he came from a strict household. Blamed it on his smothering mother and militant father. I figured that was that and felt sorry for the guy.

Fast forward to when I was nineteen, after my brother went off to college. Gerald, out of the blue, stopped by my parents' house looking for him, unaware he had moved. That should have been a red flag for me. But, since they were friends, I invited him into the house and treated him like, you know, a friend."

"Sure."

"It turned out we had a lot in common music-wise, and Gerald and I became friendly over our similar interests in certain bands, despite his off-putting behavior. I was older and thought I could handle myself, so I felt less intimidated by his bizarre quirks. Also, I was hard pressed to maintain our relationship on good terms because he was old enough to buy me and my friends alcohol." Nick exhaled. "But as I got to know him, new peculiarities began to emerge… things that worried me regardless of his size. Things you hear about in serial killer documentaries when they're evolving into the lunatics they become."

"Like what?"

"Every time he would come over to my apartment, he would ask my girlfriend for a hug." Lexi drew back a step at the word *girlfriend*. "He was after that press you get against the breasts—"

There was a hardness in Lexi's tone when she interjected, "I know the type. The key is to wear layers or be holding something you're eating on a plate. You stand away from anything you can place your dish down on and eat with your hands. It's fail-proof."

Nick paused a moment. Lexi searched his hazy features for having made herself appear paranoid.

"Sounds like you've dealt with your fair share of pervs?"

"I have." Lexi at once felt she exposed herself and was quick to cover her tracks. "I mean, every girl does at some point."

Nick quieted a moment and continued. "Well, I wish we had your advice back when."

Lexi made no comment.

"Anyway, my girlfriend just ended up staying in my room when he'd come over and I would go somewhere with him to keep him away from her and the apartment—"

"Were his stop-bys random?"

"Yeah."

"Did he ask where she was?"

"He did, every single time, and it got quite annoying."

"What would you tell him?"

"Whatever excuse I could come up with."

"Like what?"

"She's not dressed. She's in the shower. Stuff like that."

Lexi squeezed her fist. "You shouldn't have said those things."

"Why?"

"You were reinforcing his head fantasies."

"Holy shit... I think you're right. He had this thing where he would drool at random and wipe it on his shirt. It was nasty. You think he was thinking of her? I just thought it was a jaw alignment condition because of his overbite."

"Nope. He was fantasizing about your girlfriend in the next room and what he'd like to do to her."

"That's disturbing."

"Did he ever try to come over when you

weren't home and she was?"

"Not that I'm aware of."

"You should ask her when you get home."

"Oh, we don't live together anymore. I don't even talk to her."

"Sorry," Lexi said with exaggerated care.

"No, don't sweat it. I've been over her for a while."

Lexi's fist opened, her hand tingling. "Well, you can tell your current girlfriend my plate trick? It'll work against touchy-feely jerkoffs. Always does."

"Not necessary. I wouldn't tolerate a Gerald today. I was young and naive then. Even if I had a girlfriend, I wouldn't let a Gerald into my house, much less near her."

Lexi stroked her hair with her relaxing hand. *He's perfect.* "You were telling me what his new quirks were that led you to believe he was a serial killer in the making?"

"Yeah. So, he had this relationship with his mom that bordered on inappropriate."

"Ewww."

"Right, a love-hate relationship. Right in line with the serial killer Ed Kemper."

"Huh."

"Apparently, his dad had taken off, tired of his mom's extreme laziness and appetite for overeating. Gerald felt obligated to take care of his mother, even though her obese condition was reversible and her own fault. Gerald would complain to me that she'd get fatter and fatter and lazier and lazier, and I would tell him to show her some tough love. He couldn't bring himself to do it. And she relied on him to do everything, right down to giving her a bath and paying all the bills. He was worn out; you could see it behind those thick glasses of his. He was on the verge of snapping, most definitely. He just could not bring himself to challenge her. And I'm positive it was because his mother was also his girlfriend."

"That's disgusting."

"I know. It's why he was so awkward toward women. What worried me more than anything else was that they lived on a farm with a bunch of animals—"

Lexi touched Nick's arm and was quick to retract her hand, having touched him without thinking. "I know where this is going, and let's not."

"You're right, let's not."

"Hey, I wanted to ask..."

"Yeah, shoot?"

"Did you see a body in the road on the drive here, in the canyon?"

"No. I did see a van on fire."

The lights in the store came back on, stealing the two's attention towards the ceiling.

"Yay, Grandpa. The lights are back," said Candice.

Lexi smiled at the jumping little blonde-haired girl holding on to her grandfather's hand and found herself getting jealous it was not her hand she was holding.

"She's adorable, isn't she?" Lexi asked Nick.

"Yeah, she's a cutie pie."

Without another word, Lexi headed over to the girl, Nick a few steps behind her.

Candice had on a pink jacket, blue overalls, a white undershirt with a tiny pink bow at the top, and white and pink sneakers. Her face was rounded, smooth, with fat cheeks, like a doll. Most of her silky blonde hair was tucked into her jacket. Her bangs were trimmed evenly across her golden white forehead. She met Lexi's eyes in her approach. A less reserved girl shined out of her light blue gaze.

Lexi had seen Candice eye the Blow Pops.

Kneeling down, she asked, "Candice, would you like a sucker for being a brave little girl?"

Candice eyed the candy, then her grandfather, who gave her a hip nudge to answer.

She looked at Lexi. "Yes."

Her innocent soft-as-a-feather voice melted Lexi's heart. "It's okay?" Lexi asked Greg.

"Yeah. Normally, we don't let her have candy this late." Candice's eyes looked in the direction of her grandfather's legs, her head not moving, like she was getting away with a crime if she just remained muted.

"I'll get you back, Bhavin," Lexi said.

The clerk was clutching his light and preoccupied with outside. "No worries; she can have a candy for free."

"Thank you, Bhavin. What do you say to the charitable gentleman?"

Candice shied into her grandfather's hip. "Thank you."

"Yes, you are welcome."

"What flavor would you like?" Lexi asked.

Candice scanned the colors. "The red one."

"Great choice."

Lexi brought the sucker to her. Her tiny fingers took the stem as she watched Lexi. "Thank you, Lexi."

She said my name. "You're welcome, *Candice.*"

"Hello, Lexi, I'm Greg." The brown-and-grey-bearded stout man held out his aged hand. Lexi stood and shook it with no reservation.

"Pleased to meet you, Greg. Where were you two headed?"

"Back home, to Napa." Greg patted his granddaughter's head and looked at Lexi and Nick. "I was telling Bhavin he should carry our products in his store. Our family owns Valley View Vineyard. We specialize in wine, beer, and spirits. We have the finest selection in all of Southern California when it comes to taste and overall quality. We have a hundred and twenty acres of property in the soul center of wine country. We are in most retailers; you might have seen our label. We have the seal of approval on every bottle from the Cork Masters Association of America, and we have seventy-eight gold medals to our name. We're launching—"

Lexi was confused how she got stuck in a sales pitch. "Not... not to interrupt you, but I don't drink."

"Even wine?" He seemed embarrassed for

her.

"No." Lexi shook her head. "Nothing."

"Let me get you a card. Your friends and family will thank you."

Lexi looked at Nick with an expression that read, "Is this person for real?" He buttoned his bottom heavy lip to keep from laughing. Lexi glanced at Bhavin, who was staring out the window, clearly frightened by the story Nick had shared of the clown killer.

"Here we are," Greg said with a jovial smile.

Lexi took the card, her mind racing for an excuse to avoid the continuation of his conversational advertisement.

Vivid flashes illuminated the windows. Candice gripped her grandfather's leg, her sucker hanging on the verge of dropping to the floor. Lexi wanted to take her in her arms.

"It's only lightning, Candice." Lexi knelt down and rubbed her back.

Candice tried to keep her eyes open; however, the rumbling emanating from beneath their feet would not let her.

"It's okay. It's only thunder. It can't hurt you." The ground shaking subsided. "See?"

The girl's eyes opened on Lexi, and she re-gripped her sucker. Her grandfather reached down and patted her on the cheek twice, harder than was appropriate, saying, "She's resilient."

It took everything for Lexi not to yell, *Gentle with her!*

As I was saying, our vineyard..."

Lexi tuned the man out, staying next to Candice.

BANG! A sound like a metal trashcan colliding with the stockroom's roll door sprang Lexi to her feet with a startled jolt.

"What was that?" asked Greg, quicker than the rest.

Lexi put a shielding hand behind her for Candice. The five stared at the stockroom entrance, listening for a pin drop. A second banging sound from the same location shuddered the group and sent Candice into her grandfather's hip, mumbling, "I want to go."

A second later, the store was thrown into complete darkness.

"Grandpa!"

Not missing a beat, Bhavin turned on his flashlight. Nick and Greg added their cell phone lights. The store was a mass of eerie, trembling shadows. Lexi kept her eyes on the stockroom door, prepared to do whatever it took to protect the girl. A mad wind fire-hosed the wall of windows at their backs. Gust after gust of gale force pressure moaned at the seams to push the front doors open. When the wind died down, the rain did the opposite.

"Bhavin, you're positive the back doors are locked?" Nick asked.

"...Yes."

"Why did you hesitate?"

"I was thinking."

"We have to make sure," Lexi said, taking wary steps towards the stockroom with her veiled scissors in hand.

"Wait, the police are coming," yelled Bhavin, loud enough to project into the stockroom.

Red and blue lights rotated where the invisible road extended.

"Can we leave?" Candice mumbled, stuffed into her grandfather's coat.

"Candice, knock it off," replied Greg, with no patience for her jitters, nor his own.

Rubbing Candice's back, Lexi pulled half her observation off the stockroom door to speak into the little girl's ear. "We'll get out of here soon; don't worry. 'Kay?"

Candice's nose exhaled her skepticism in a

partial look back.

The officer pulled into the station and coasted by the wall of pale lit occupants waving and calling for assistance. In turn, they were greeted by a blinding search light probing their identities.

Lexi swung a look at the stockroom door, her worst fear realized. The killer *was* nearby, a likelihood re-affirmed when the patrol car crept out of sight to round the perimeter of the building.

"Where is the policeman going?" Candice said, tugging on her grandfather's coat.

"Candice, knock it off. They'll be back," Greg said.

While Candice was burying her head in her grandfather's coat, Lexi's facial language shared with the others what they were already dreading. The four watched the entryway door to the stockroom with peaked nerves. In the play of shadows, the door seemed to have a gap, as if someone was peering out of it.

For a time, no one moved, only stared and listened by the front entrance, waiting for the patrol car to make its return. As ample minutes passed in slow motion and the inner concerns of Lexi and the others played tricks on them within the shadows, Lexi perceived a definite movement in the gap of the door. Her eyes widened as the door parted, twitching from the strain of investigation in improper lighting. Her voice went to sound an alarm and was seized when the store lights turned on and the stockroom door was found shut tight. Lexi cocked her head at the impossible illusion, her eyes watering at the sight. She put four fingers to her sudden aching temple, rubbing the pulsing spot.

"Do you have a headache?" Lexi looked down at Candice and frowned in confusion. They were holding hands. *When?* In a startled look around, she saw Bhavin, Nick, and Greg talking to a male officer in the well-lit and open stockroom. Lexi's heart went out of control, and she began to convulse from dizziness. None of it made any sense, and she couldn't breathe because of it.

"Grandpa, something's wrong with Lexi."

Lexi gasped, dropping to her knees to find breath. She fell over into a rack when no air came. She heard Candice cry her name, and then in a blink of an eye, it was quiet and blacker than black.

FIFTEEN

When Lexi came to, she was slow to rise. She had a minor headache, and her vision was in and out of focus. Sitting up on her forearms, she felt a weight on her legs. Her hair fell over her face, but she was too weak to care. She was back on the heated blanket that had been moved to the front section of the store. Candice was draped over her thighs, fast asleep and lightly snoring. A groggy stupor clouded Lexi's thoughts as she attempted to recount how she got where she was.

"Feeling better?" Nick was resting in an elevated position with his back to a makeshift recliner of packaged toilet paper.

"Yeah. What happened?" She yawned.

"You passed out."

"I did?" she asked, eyeing the ground through her hair.

"Yep. You gave everyone quite the scare."

"I did?" Her eyes lifted and lowered.

Lexi had the sense she was in a dream.

"The officer looked you over and said your vitals were okay and that you likely dropped from exhaustion. He is having an ambulance come to look at you."

"No, that's okay." Her vision was clearing.

"I don't think you have a choice."

Lexi pursed her lips and exhaled, pushing forward on her shoulders in a stretch. "Sorry I scared everyone."

"Why are you sorry? We are just glad you are okay."

She attempted a smile, thinking about fixing her hair, but she had no real intention of doing so.

"Why don't you go back to sleep? I'll wake you up when the paramedics arrive."

She shook her shaggy head. "I can't sleep. What time is it?"

Nick retrieved his cell. "Three-ten."

"When did the officer leave?"

"'Bout twenty minutes ago."

"Where are Bhavin and Greg?" She looked

around with the sudden realization they were nowhere in sight.

"Sleeping." Nick gestured his head toward the rack supporting the back of his recliner.

Lexi shook her head in a downcast stare. *I'm falling to pieces.* "It's weird…"

"What is?"

Lexi's forehead sat heavy over her eyes. "I'm missing time."

"How so?"

"Last thing I remember is that I thought I saw someone in the stockroom when the lights were out. I went to say something…and then the lights were on, and you all were talking to an officer."

Lexi gave a pained expression at the floor.

"Stress can affect your ability to remember. Your body has to recover from what you've been through."

Lexi peered at him. "I feel like I'm dreaming."

"Yeah, 'cause you need rest. Lexi, you really should try to get some sleep."

She put in the effort to brush back her hair. "I'm fine."

"If you must be stubborn…" Nick said, standing. He went to the refrigeration section and returned with two sparkling grape caffeinated drinks. "It'll give you a boost."

"Thanks." The liquid reminded Lexi that she no longer had the pressure to pee. *Did I go to the restroom?* Her memory flashed a small room, florescent bulbs, a white sink, and an empty soap dish and paper towel dispenser. Her eyes oscillated at the flashes, unable to verify the bathroom was in the store and not another location, at another time.

Lexi sipped the energy drink, thinking. The sour grape soda flavor was pleasing to her parched throat.

"So, Lexi..."

She looked at Nick and her right eye twitched, insisting she rub it to stop.

"What do you do for a living?"

"I'm a student at Red Falls University."

"Red Falls, in Redlands?"

"Yeah."

"My friend Andrew goes to Red Falls."

"Oh, yeah?"

"Yeah. It's a stunning campus."

"It is." Lexi sipped her drink.

"What are you majoring in?"

"Law."

"Wow. Well, if I ever should require a lawyer, I know who to call."

"Do." She phrased her reply in such a way that she thought it made her look desperate.

"I will." Nick smiled, easing her thoughts on the matter.

He likes me. He really does like me.

"What got you interested in law?"

Lexi paused, her heart in unison. She reflected on just how honest she wanted to be. *Tell him. What do you have to lose? If he doesn't understand, fuck him. He doesn't deserve you.* The rain gained on her ears and intruded on her thoughts with a wailing wind gust.

Lexi looked out the windows at the cold dark night and drifted back into her mind when Nick said sincerely, "You don't have to tell me. It's no big deal." His tone was honest and caring.

Lexi faced him, her palpable suffering already on the table. Pent-up tears from childhood to the present moment ran down her cheeks. She was gambling for her happiness. For her sanity. For her life in general. It was time not to feel ashamed of what she had no control over. Now was the opportunity to put her trust in someone else of the opposite sex, what her therapist Vanessa had worked with her for countless hours to achieve. A wholesome, functional relationship of complete understanding. An understanding of boundaries and expectations. That the foundation of a relationship with her was, at its core, built on patience.

Lexi looked off and spoke low between sniffs. "I was eight. My parents took me on a trip to Mammoth. I got lost on a hiking trail in the mountains. I remember it got dark out and I was freezing to death. I could hear my parents and others calling. I called back, but it was no use. The area was too dense with trees." Lexi released a tormented exhale. "I came across two men..." She paused to the point where Nick didn't think she would continue. "...They were sitting by a fire. I was numb to where my bones stung." Lexi shivered. "They terrified me... their faces... but I couldn't say no to the warmth. I was so cold I couldn't resist." Lexi could hear her heart beating. She took a shallow breath and looked straight at Nick. His expression was acute with apprehension. Lexi could see his chest rise and fall faster with every concluding word. "I'll leave it at... they hurt me terribly."

"Shit, Lexi—"

"Don't cuss." She motioned at Candice.

Nick lowered his voice. "Sorry." He shook his

head. "Girl, that's heavy."

Lexi wiped her tears. "It's the reason I went into law. I want to punish the wicked men who abuse women and children."

"Admirable cause," he said, stuck in an aftershock. "Do you mind me asking, were these animals ever caught?"

Lexi looked out the store's window and drew her lips into her mouth, about to lose herself in a crying fit.

"So... I hear the bar is five thousand dollars every time you have to take it. Is that true?"

She looked at Nick, who was drinking his beverage like the prior topic never happened. Lexi's lips reappeared, and the want to lose it faded. It took a cough to get the trauma out of her voice. "It's expensive. You have the study materials, the exam, your filing fees, the interest it adds to your loan. I don't know if it's five thousand dollars exactly; it's high, though."

"Yeah, it is. How much do you have in student debt?"

"Now, or in the end?"

"The latter."

"About two hundred grand."

Nick about came out of his toilet paper

recliner to fake a heart attack. "What?" he yelled, in a whisper.

Lexi couldn't help but laugh. "Yeah, it's seven years of college."

"Translation. You're in debt forever."

"Pretty much."

"Dang. That's insane. Sounds like you should be a lawyer against student loans."

"I should." Lexi brightened. "Nick, what do you do for a living?"

"I'm a veterinarian assistant at Paw Pals in Palm Springs. I plan to go back to school to get my veterinarian medicine degree. I have a year and half, I think, left to graduate. I'll have to look at my credits again."

"You're an animal lover?"

"I am. I have two dogs. A golden retriever and a hound mix. My goal is to start a rescue. Well, we'll see what happens after school. You have any pets?"

"No, my dorm doesn't allow pets. I would if I could; I adore dogs."

"That's a bummer."

"Eh." Lexi shrugged. "It's temporary."

"True."

"Who's watching your dogs?" Lexi probed.

"A dog sitter. You want to see a picture of my

babies?"

"Yeah."

Nick walked to Lexi, getting close enough to touch shoulders with her. She eyed him up and down with thoughts of the future. *Ahhh. I can't believe this.* The pictures on his phone were of his dogs cuddled up in their adjoining beds. Both were covered to the neck in blankets and looking at him take the picture with the cutest calendar-worthy expressions.

"Awe, they're adorable."

"Thank you. The golden's name is Shyann, and the hound mix, Baxter."

"Those names are fantastic, Nick."

"Thanks."

Lexi handed him back his phone, and Nick returned to his seat.

"They're my babies," he said, eyeing his phone a last second before putting the device back in his pocket. "Look, uh… I was going to ask you something, and tell me if this is too forward."

"Okay." Lexi's heart began thumping.

"Would you maybe want to attend my brother's wedding with me? Assuming you feel up to it?"

"*Yeah, I'll go.*"

"*Yeah?*"

"Yeah, I'd love to," Lexi said, blushing with a wide beaming smile.

"Awesome. That would be great. It'll be boring, but with you there it—"

The rev of a car's engine was heard. In a fraction of a second, Lexi observed the store explode. Flying glass was everywhere. A violent rush of wind shoved everything in sight. In her instinctive reaction to protect herself, she watched a squad car's bumper smash into Nick's face and torso. He was wrenched underneath the vehicle, which drove into the racks behind him and into the refrigeration section, colliding in a pounding shriek of metal.

Time went in slow motion. Lexi saw the broken-down wall of windows, felt the polar wind filling the air along with a burning sensation on her legs. Candice was crawling onto her chest, screaming. And then, there was Nick, mangled on the floor, his pooling blood turning the dispersed toilet paper a deep red. Paralyzed, Lexi half expected to wake up from a dream; however, it was the clown in the driver's seat of the squad car that prompted Lexi to get up, dream or no dream.

With eyes bulging out of her skull, Lexi

clutched Candice to her, the little girl's screams deafening her right ear. Using a hand for balance, she got to her feet and slipped to a kneeling position from dizziness and unsteady limbs. Candice's fingers dug into her back to hold on as Lexi whined in desperation, begging her body for cooperation. The panic she was in gave a quick recovery to her feet.

Somehow, Lexi maintained a run to the stockroom. She moved to shut the door and saw the keys to Bhavin's office were dangling in the lock. She peeked around the wall at the clown doing something inside the unit and decided to make a dash for the fortified partition. Her legs sprang into action without a second thought. She twisted the keys in the lock. The door came open, and Lexi locked herself and Candice inside.

She pressed a hand against the child's head to lean her mouth away from her ear. *Don't pass out. Don't pass out. You can't pass out.* Lexi couldn't breathe. She was convulsing on legs threatening to give out. *Don't pass out; you can't.*

Lexi's thoughts shook with her. *He can't get in. He can't get in.* She tried desperately to focus on her breath, a task coming off impossible with Candice splitting her eardrum.

"Grandpa!"

Lexi shielded Candice from the clown by facing her toward the back wall. Her grandfather was somewhere underneath the fallen racks with Bhavin, likely injured or dead. Lexi froze in shock at the sight of Nick, his entire face caved in. The gore was so extreme that it didn't look real. His face appeared to be made of clay and fake blood. *Ahhh!* Lexi began gasping for air, falling back against a counter.

Don't pass out. Please, don't pass out. Lexi cried in her head, not knowing what to do in the screaming disorder. She couldn't let him get the girl. She couldn't. She'd kill him first.

It was then Lexi glanced at the clown watching her from the driver's seat. Walter Harris had rolled down his window to enjoy the show of cornered terror. His ugly face smiled at their helplessness. For whatever reason, Lexi's panic was gone, replaced by unadulterated hatred. Her funny face withdrew as her breath came back to her. She was like a bull, breathing in snorts, as if in preparation to charge a matador. Seeing only red, she bared her teeth at him, staring back in a challenge that read, *Let's see who can kill who first, motherfucker.*

SIXTEEN

The clown threw his head back in a chuckle, letting Lexi know he accepted her challenge. Walter Harris kicked the blood-streaked patrol door open and stepped out onto a toppled rack covered in a disarray of merchandise. In his grimy, once white, gloved hand, was a police-issued shotgun. He walked with a silly animated gait as if he were putting on a performance for children to get laughs. Bags popped and food crunched beneath his large bare feet that were glistening a soiled black, as though he'd been walking through raw sewage. With long, cartoony strides, he made for flat ground amid the devastation.

Stepping into Nick's blood, the clown put a backwards-facing peace sign to his smeared red lips and licked his ink-stained tongue into the middle of his spread-eagle fingers. Lexi held the back of Candice's head, looking for a weapon. The little girl was no longer screaming; she was crying in heaving moans. Lexi had told her to close her eyes and not to look until she was told otherwise.

The six-foot-three clown wore a blue pom-pom costume ruffled at the neck that presented evidence of a lengthy rampage from head to toe. The bruises, cuts, tears, and handprints hinted that not all victims went down without a fight. He moved toward the partition, sizing up the thick glass with sunken misaligned eyes that were bloodshot and sallow at the yokes. His ugly face was covered in runny makeup, giving it the illusion of melting. The red hair surrounding his brain cavity was lolled over his shoulders. The sight made Lexi's stomach sick and her shakes evident. She fought not to display her vulnerability to him, but there was no shut-off valve for her overwrought nerves.

"Candice, I have to put you down."

The reluctant child fought her protector. "No, Lexi, no!"

"Candice." She put the child's face to hers, squeezing her puffy cheeks inward. "Look at me."

She shook her. "Look at me."

Candice's streaming eyes peeked open. "If you don't do as I say, he'll kill us both. Do you understand? You have to listen to me." The child choked back sobs and released her tenacious grip on Lexi. Lexi placed her under the register in a cubbyhole section meant for the waste basket. "Cover your ears and close your eyes until I tell you different."

"Lexi, where's Grandpa?" she sniveled.

"Do as I say."

Crying louder, Candice minded.

Lexi stood in a confrontational stare, taking a large vodka bottle off the back wall to use as a club. "You want a piece of me. C'mon and get it," she said, shining her clenched teeth at him.

Walter Harris clawed once at Lexi. "Meow, kitty, kitty. Come out and play." His voice did not befit his psychotic image. It was the voice of a bank teller, a dentist, a real estate agent, a grocery bagger, a normal, average everyday Joe, not the sadistic tone of a madman run amok. Somehow, its normal everyday quality was worse. Much worse, because it was no different from Lexi's parents, her friend Rachael, or her fiancé Chad, or worse yet, Candice when she would grow up. It was her own voice as well, separated merely by gender.

"Fuck you." Lexi gave him the finger.

"Free hugs?" The clown opened his arms, waving her in with his fingers to accept his offer.

"You're insane." She seethed between her teeth.

"I know you are, but what am I?" he said in the voice of Pee Wee Herman, complete with the high-pitched laugh.

Lexi went to say something and couldn't get the words out. The man's attitude was too random and crazy for her to communicate with. The clown walked up to the glass slowly, observing her breasts and licking his lips. Lexi got into a combative crouch, standing her ground for the opportunity to whack him one good, say he got past the partition. The clown examined the trim of the glass, his shotgun directed limply at the floor.

His eyes traveled down to Lexi, his blank, dark, penetrating stare going through her. "Tell you what ...you give me the kid and I'll let you live. You don't, and ...you're in for a special treat. Whaddaya say, pilgrim?"

Lexi's funny face appeared—however, not from fear. She stood straight up and close to the glass. "I am going to kill you." Her eyes grew wider than they ever had. "You are going to die this morning." Her eyes bore into his uneven pair, devoid of any other outcome.

They stared at each other, neither blinking or moving a muscle.

"Game on, bitch." The clown's shotgun swung up to the glass as he stepped back, the barrel making contact. Lexi got onto the floor next to Candice. Walter's real eyebrows pushed his painted, black arched eyebrows upward. "Last chance?"

"Candice, cover your ears."

The clown swayed his body back and forth and sang, "Why can't we be friends, why can't we be friends, why can't we be friends, why can't we be friends."

"Lexi," Candice cried.

"Candice, cover your ears, now!"

The clown whistled. "Yoo-hoo, kiddo. Want some candy?"

"Don't you talk to her!"

"Shut up. I'm in charge." Walter walked up and hit the glass with a hammer fist, leaving an oily residue on the glass.

Candice screamed.

"I'm in charge!" The clown had lost control

and reclaimed himself with the self-awareness he had prior. "Lady, you're in-corrig-ible." The clown's lips and teeth formed out of the mix of red, black, and white paint. His teeth were discolored from the rain, having leaked makeup into his mouth. He stretched his smile to a horrific extent, painting a picture of his disturbing desires. "You and the girl are mine."

"That's what you think."

"That's what I know, bitch."

Lexi's shakes were increasing. She knew she would have to get at him soon.

The boom from the flaring shotgun was ear-piercing. Items from the shelves fell onto the floor, along with Lexi, who covered her ears, feeling the impact radiate down her spine. She looked at the gossamer web-shaped break in the glass. The partition was holding, at least so far. One of the items that fell on the floor was a cell phone she hadn't seen. She went to it and dialed 911 with fumbling fingers. With her hands occupied, she couldn't protect her ears from the second blast.

"They'll never make it!" the clown yelled, hammering a fist on the still-holding glass.

"911, what's—"

"The clown is here!" The third blast broke

bottles on the ground. Lexi's ears started to ring. Candice's screams and the 911 operator were one annoying intrusion on her ability to speak. "We are at the Fuel n' Snack off Taft Highway. Hurry! He's armed with a shotgun! He's trying to kill us!"

"Ma'am, officers are en route."

After the fourth shot, Lexi's ears could no longer take the abuse. She put the phone in her pocket and looked at the battered glass on the verge of giving in. The clown geared up for a fifth shot. The shotgun clicked but did not fire. The clown hollered at the gun before throwing it down in a rage.

"Ha, ha. What's a matter, your gun run out of bullets?" Lexi mocked, despite her dazed state. "The police are coming; you better hurry and get us," she taunted, holding the neck of the vodka bottle again.

"Lexi, no!" Candice screamed.

Walter rushed the window, pounding on it in an idiotic frenzy. Then the clown went away. Lexi stood to see what his plan was. Her eyes opened wide. She dragged the screaming Candice out from beneath the table and carried her to the door of Bhavin's office. The clown was getting back into the squad car. "That's right; you'd better run," she said, holding the back of the little girl's head.

"Lexi, your leg," Candice said, pointing.

Lexi looked down and at that instant felt a sharp pain. A huge piece of glass was sticking out of her right calf. Her trembling hand went to pull it out, and she was alarmed to find her hand was covered in blood from cuts. Gripping the tail end of the glass shard, she gave three preparatory breaths and yanked. "Oh my—!" Her head hit the wall behind her, her eyes shedding tears. The twinge was brutal, and she nearly dropped Candice because of it. An excruciating burning sensation rose and fell from her calf to her neck, promising that if she did that again, she would pass out. Lexi's fingers squirmed, "*okay, okay*" at the wound, signaling her compliance if it would only stop hurting. When the tingling poker stabs wore off enough to open her eyes, the punctured meat took a back seat to a more pressing circumstance.

The squad car had backed up and was directed at the partition. The clown's mouth made an "O" at Lexi. *He's going to ram us!* Her eyes twitched as her brain went into action for what to do. In a panic, she searched for the keys, forgetting where she set them down, assuming they didn't fall on the floor. *Where are they?* She screamed in her head for the keys and the cops.

The squad car tires squealed. Lexi screamed, with a voice capable of blowing out her windpipe.

It was over and she knew it. She had sealed herself and Candice's fate. "I'm sorry, Candice," she said, pressing her forehead to the little girl's temple. Lexi heard another squeal of the tires and glanced up. The vehicle was stuck on a rack. With a quick inhale of breath, she kept looking. She spotted the keys by the register. Lexi hobbled over while the squad car went into reverse, taking two racks with it. She snagged the keys and got to the lock. She heard the car come to an abrupt halt and switch into acceleration. The car peeled out. Lexi dropped the keys at the sound. The patrol car's engine was building in her ears, getting closer and closer and closer.

Lexi turned the lock, and the door sprang open. The partition smashed inward. Disoriented, she lunged her and Candice into the adjoining wall, falling a few feet short of the stockroom. Looking up to get her bearings, she saw Bhavin was split in two. Lexi groaned at the sight. Candice went to look in that direction to catch a breath, and Lexi shielded her from the indelible horror.

Getting to her feet on one functional leg, Lexi

got dizzy and had to take a moment to avoid falling down. She felt the urge to puke and did a little in her mouth. Candice screamed bloody murder when she saw the clown get out of the cruiser. Then her crying stopped, and she went limp in Lexi's arms. Lexi hobbled the few feet to get her hand on the stockroom door.

"No, you don't," said the clown.

She was kicked in the stomach before she could turn the knob and fell right on the glass in her leg. The holler she let out was inhuman. She felt her hair being pulled, her neck ready to snap as her entire upper half was lifted from the floor. Lexi was gurgling with insufferable agony, and the sensation entering her throat from the angle of her crooked neck choked her. "Fuck you," she said, managing to spit at Walter.

The clown licked the spit off his face. "Mmm, tastes wonderful."

There was a glint of movement from Lexi's hand, and the clown looked down at it. Lexi was dropped to the floor, coughing in an attempt to breathe past the searing pain quaking her leg as she writhed in agony, squeezing the area around the glass. The clown stood over her, pulling the long, silver piece of metal out of his throat. He attempted to block the blood from spurting out. It oozed pure red between his fingers as he dropped the scissors.

Lexi's moans of agony grew into uncontrollable laughter. The clown peered down at her funny face, laughing at him as if she were possessed by the Devil himself. "Hemorrhagic shock will take effect very soon." She laughed. "In other words, I win." The clown stumbled backward. "You are funny." The clown fell, smacking the back of his skull against the buried patrol car in a dying stare at Lexi. "Very funny." She laughed and laughed.

SEVENTEEN

Radio announcer: "In the early morning hours, police identified the deceased body of suspect Walter Harris. Walter was wanted in connection with at least eleven murders. According to detectives, after killing his boss and family, including the family dog, Walter went on a random killing spree on Interstate Five dressed in a clown costume for a children's fundraiser. The identification came after a dramatic call was placed to 911 operators by an unknown female caller. Police responded to the scene to witness what they called a *mound of unadulterated carnage,* adding three additional victims to Walter's death toll. "

Radio announcer continues: "Walter Harris had taken police officer Jenkins' cruiser after an apparent struggle left the officer mortally wounded. Walter then drove the cruiser into the front of a Fuel n' Snack mini mart store off Taft Highway where three victims were found among the devastation. The victims are yet to be identified. At the present time, it is unclear as to what transpired and who ended Walter Harris's reign of terror. The serial killer was found dead with a puncture wound in his neck. Police are looking into the store's security tape for clues but are wary the storm's interference may leave them without answers. Police are hoping the female caller is still alive and will call them with information."

"We have breaking news. Police in Redlands, California have made a grisly discovery at Red Falls University."

Lexi shot a look at the radio and turned up the volume.

Radio announcer: "A custodian cleaning the campus dorms heard calls for help in one of the rooms. The custodian notified campus security, who gained entry. Two individuals were uncovered in a closet, bound, gagged, and stabbed multiple times. Among them, Rachael Greene, now deceased, and her fiancé Chad Levine, who was rushed to Redlands Lutheran Hospital and remains in critical condition. Police are looking for Lexi Peters, a student—"

Lexi clicked off the radio and cupped her mouth in shock. "How did he get to them?" she whispered, wide eyed.

Candice was waking from the nightmare that Lexi knew would scar her for the rest of her life, but she also knew that together they would find the strength to pull through anything. They were nearly home, nearly free and secure. And, best of all, Lexi had faced her fear in the process. No regression. No regret.

She caressed the little girl's silky hair.

"Lexi?" she said, coming to.

"It's alright. You're safe. We got away."

Candice quivered at the lips and began to cry, looking at Lexi.

"It's okay, it's okay." Lexi rubbed her leg.

"Where's Grandpa?" Candice whined.

"In the back."

Candice scrambled to look into the back seat of Nick's truck. The empty eyes of Greg's detached head looked back at her.

The little girl screamed, making her own funny face.

Also by Brian Lupo

Goat's Head

There are worse things than the Ones Who Dwell in the Dark…

Vince Marino is a dispirited sixteen-year-old, who is afflicted with anxiety panic disorder and an excessive fear of the dark. In his mind, he has nowhere else to turn but suicide. His one and only friend, Melissa, suggests he try hypnotherapy, which helped her deal with depression after her father's death. Desperate, Vince agrees.

In his first session, Vince recounts a terrifying experience he had three years earlier at Goat's Head, a local haunt in his small hometown of Yucaipa. He and his then best friends, Jarrod and Ethan, went to retrieve a goat's skull that was said to hang on a barn owned by a presumed dead cult leader, Blackie Wilson. Here he encounters the Ones Who Dwell in the Dark.

When Bruce McGrail, Vince's hypnotherapist, returns home that evening from work, he finds his house has been broken into by an unwelcomed visitor. A visitor that won't stay away. Bruce and his family's nightmare begins as they start to realize that there might be a connection between what now stalks them and Vince's encounter with the Ones Who Dwell in the Dark.

ISBN: 978-1729619841

available at

amazon   **BARNES&NOBLE**